MESMERIA
BRIGHTLAND

The Dark
Green Tunnel

Books by Allan W. Eckert

The Winning of America Series
The Frontiersmen
Wilderness Empire
The Conquerors
The Wilderness War
Gateway to Empire

Other Books
The Great Auk
The Silent Sky
A Time of Terror
Wild Season
The Dreaming Tree
The King Snake
The Crossbreed
Bayou Backwaters
The Court-Martial of Daniel Boone
Blue Jacket
In Search of a Whale
The Owls of North America
Tecumseh! (Drama)
The Hab Theory
The Wading Birds of North America
Incident at Hawk's Hill
Savage Journey
Song of the Wild
Whattizzit?
Johnny Logan
The Dark Green Tunnel

The Dark
Green Tunnel

by Allan W. Eckert

Illustrated by David Wiesner

Little, Brown and Company
BOSTON   TORONTO

TEXT COPYRIGHT © 1984 BY ALLAN W. ECKERT

ILLUSTRATIONS COPYRIGHT © 1984 BY DAVID WIESNER

FIRST EDITION

Library of Congress Cataloging in Publication Data

Eckert, Allan W.
   The dark green tunnel.

   Summary: Three children in the Florida Everglades find
an entrance to another world which is peopled with
centaurs, gnomes, a wizard, and a wicked king, and where
they experience both great danger and great joy.
   [1. Fantasy] I. Wiesner, David, ill.   II. Title.
PZ7.E1978Dar 1983   [Fic]   83-25548
ISBN 0-316-20881-7

MV

*Published simultaneously in Canada
by Little, Brown & Company (Canada) Limited*

PRINTED IN THE UNITED STATES OF AMERICA

Dedicated
to the memory of
the creator of
The Chronicles of Narnia —
C. S. LEWIS
— whose charming tales
have the ability
to keep us
forever young

Contents

The Dark
Green Tunnel

1

William's Secret

ONLY FIFTEEN MINUTES had passed since Barnaby and his cousin, William, left the dock in the little motorboat. Now, as the waterway they were following began to narrow in a way that seemed menacing, Barnaby was having some very serious second thoughts about this whole venture. Nevertheless, it was pride that caused his expression to remain frozen in a look of mild interest so he would not betray his growing fear.

It wasn't apprehension inspired by his cousin's operation of the boat that was having this effect on Barnaby. Actually, William was doing quite a commendable job. He wasn't showing off at all (as Barnaby had expected he would) and, with the handle of the outboard motor gripped tightly in his hand, he was guiding the boat very skillfully. He was turning and weaving carefully, avoiding the islands that seemed to be closing in on them more and more. Soon they were following a waterway as broad as a street between forbidding mangrove swamp shorelines. Still, the water kept narrowing until it was only twice as wide as their boat. The black branches of the mangrove trees seemed to be reaching out for them, with thick, heavy leaves that would, Barnaby thought, enfold them in a smothering blanket.

Somehow Barnaby managed to keep his expression from changing, hiding the fact that he was suddenly, pointlessly, asking himself some very scary questions. What, he thought, am I doing in this dinky boat, heading into the Everglades, the largest swamp in North America? Why am I putting my life in the hands of a cousin not quite two years older than me, when I only met him for the first time yesterday? What if we hit a submerged log and sink? What if some wild animal — a big alligator, maybe — attacks us? Why didn't I stay back at the dock with Lara? (Lara was his twin sister.)

When they had first left the dock in front of William's house in Everglades City, Barnaby had been excited about the boat trip. It had all the promise of being an exciting little adventure. They had putt-putted out the nearby mouth of the Barron River into a large open bay dotted with islands. William called it Chokoloskee Bay and it was located on the coast almost at the southwestern tip of Florida. This was where the great Everglades swamp of Florida met the Gulf of Mexico — where the tangled jungle of mangrove trees separated into a multitude of islands. In fact, they even called this area the Ten Thousand Islands and it was like nothing Barnaby had seen before.

For the first five or ten minutes of their boat ride the clear blue-green water had been fairly open and occasionally Barnaby caught glimpses of starfish and shells on the submerged sandbars they crossed. But then, as his cousin headed the boat southeastward, they encountered many more islands and William had begun weaving a path through them. The deeper they penetrated, the less open water there was. As the boat came closer to the islands, Barnaby was surprised to discover that they were not the sort of islands he expected them to be. For one thing the mangrove trees did not grow out of the ground. They sprang up right from the water on weirdly twisted roots coated with oysters. These same reddish-colored roots, above the surface, formed an unbelievable interlocking tangle from which rose the gnarled trunks of the mangrove trees.

Soon the boat was moving rapidly through what had become little more than a maze of interconnecting water passages. In a very short time Barnaby had become so confused by the winding course they had taken that he could never find his way back to Everglades City by himself. That was when he had begun getting afraid.

The sudden slowing of the boat caused Barnaby to shake the thoughts away and look around. The particular passage they were following had now become so narrow and twisting that occasional branches were scraping against the sides of the boat with shrill screeching sounds. To Barnaby, these sounds were like a warning for the boys to go back. He didn't like it at all and was about to swallow his pride and tell his cousin to turn around when abruptly the narrow passage opened into a little hidden bay about double the size of a baseball diamond. The water here was different. It had become very dark in color; not muddied, but a clear darkness, like the color of tea that has been brewed to a rich deep brown. William turned off the motor and they drifted quietly.

It was a lovely area, yet it touched Barnaby with an eerie sense. Snow white egrets perched on the mangrove roots or waded about in shallows on long spindly legs. Every now and then one would thrust its head quickly toward the dark water and spear a small fish on its sharp beak. A turtle came to the surface near the boat, stared at them a moment and then dived out of sight. Not far from them a large dark bird stood on a bare branch overhanging the water, its wings held outstretched. Barnaby pointed at it.

"Isn't that an anhinga?"

William stared at him in surprise and nodded. "Yes, but how did you know?"

Barnaby was pleased with himself. "I've seen pictures in books. I do a lot of reading about animals in the school library. I remember things. But," he added, "there are a lot of things here I don't recognize. Like that turtle we just saw. I've seen lots of turtles, but never one that looked like that."

"It was a diamondback terrapin," William said. "We've got lots of animals here you've never seen in the wild before."

"Like what?"

William smiled a trifle maliciously. "Well, besides the turtles there are frogs and lizards and snakes and all kinds of fish. And raccoons and otters and armadillos and bobcats."

"Snakes? Bobcats?" Barnaby's eyes widened.

"Oh, sure. That's nothing. We've also got panthers."

"*Panthers!*"

"Uh huh. Don't see 'em very often," the older boy replied, still smiling, "but they're around. Bears, too."

"Bears?" Barnaby's voice squeaked and he was immediately embarrassed.

His cousin nodded, but then the little trace of meanness left him and his expression softened. "Don't worry," he said. "They're pretty scarce. You'd be lucky to see just one if you came here every day for a year."

They lapsed into silence then, content to watch the birds wading in the shallows. Or at least Barnaby was. William, on the other hand, seemed to be considering something. Then he nodded.

"Listen, Barnaby," he said, "if you can keep your trap shut, I think I'll show you something special. A secret."

"Really? What?"

Instead of answering, William pulled the cord and started the motor again. Several of the birds squawked and leaped into graceful flight on powerful wings. They disappeared over the low trees. William headed the boat toward the far side of the bay. When they got there, Barnaby could see that the mangrove trees were much older and even more gnarled than those they had seen in Chokoloskee Bay. A certain amount of soil had built up about their roots, mostly from decomposed leaves, and so it looked more like a real shoreline. However, he was quite sure that this black material would be very mucky. A little thread of fear bloomed in him as he imagined that William might want him to step out of the boat onto it and that it might be like quicksand — able to swallow him up without trace. Instead, William turned the boat to the right and followed the dense vegetation of the shoreline to an area where the mangroves bowed inward, forming a crescent curve. It looked as if some great creature with a mouth about twelve feet wide had taken a bite out of the shore.

"Here we are," William said, cutting off the motor.

"Where's here?"

"Don't you see anything?" William snickered. When

Barnaby shook his head, the older boy continued. "Well, neither does anybody else who comes here. Not many ever come, but those who do never even see it. Dad found it."

"See *what?*" Barnaby persisted, growing irritated at the way William was being so mysterious. "What did Uncle Danny find?"

"Well," his cousin said, "I have to explain something to you first. There are lots of little bays like this one. Most of them are fed by freshwater streams running in from the upper Everglades, and then the water in these little bays runs out into bigger bays, like Chokoloskee, and then from there out into the Gulf. Sometimes two or three streams will run into one little bay like this, but usually it's only one. Dad found this bay once when he was out fishing. Right away he noticed that there didn't seem to be any kind of a feeder creek emptying into it."

"Couldn't it just be a sort of backwater, pushed in by the tide?" Barnaby asked.

"That's probably what most people would think if they thought about it at all," William said. "But then it would be a saltwater bay. Dad tasted it and found it wasn't very salty at all, so he figured the water in this little bay had to come from somewhere else — an underwater spring or some kind of a feeder creek or something. He followed the edge of the mangroves until he came to this place where the shore took a sudden curve inward and that's when he noticed there was a little current running out into the bay."

"A current?" Barnaby stared at the dense screen of leaves and branches and could see no opening. "From where?"

"Right from the center of this little sort of crescent shape. That's when he pushed the nose of the boat in there." William pointed at the centermost portion of the indentation in the mangroves. "It's so well hidden you can't see it yet, but there's a feeder creek behind those mangroves, just like Dad suspected. You have to drive the boat in right through those branches and then you're inside. It's really a terrific secret place — like being in a tunnel. Want to see it?"

Barnaby hesitated. He was afraid but didn't want to admit it.

"C'mon," William coaxed, "you're not afraid, are you? I've been in there a lot. It's neat!"

Barnaby opened his mouth to say no, but that was not what came out.

"Okay," he said.

2

William's Big Brown Bird

LARA was sitting on the edge of the dock with her bare toes only an inch or two above the water, feeling left out and rather sorry for herself. She had been waiting for over an hour and now very much wished she had gone with the boys. Writing the postcard to Mother and Father in Chicago had taken only a short time and after that there wasn't much to do by herself, so she had returned to the dock. It was very still and peaceful here and it took a little while for her to realize there were living things nearby.

The first creatures she spied were across the Barron River from her — several large brown pelicans perched above the water on the low branches of the mangrove trees. She watched them for a long while and then five more of the huge birds glided into view in single file. They were so close to the water that once or twice the

outermost tips of their long wing feathers barely touched the water. They flapped great wings simultaneously for a few seconds, then glided again just over the surface and disappeared around the bend upriver.

Somewhat later a group of gulls wheeled past overhead, laughing noisily as they moved out of sight. Closer to the dock a grasshopper leaped off a tall weed on shore and landed in the water. It kicked a few times, heading back toward land, but a large fish flashed beneath it. There was a brief swirl and faint popping sound and the grasshopper was gone. Only expanding rings on the surface marked where it had been. It had all happened so fast Lara could hardly believe it. A little shiver ran up her spine.

After another ten minutes, a small wake in the surface

only twenty yards away caught the girl's attention and she thought at first it was the river current spreading past a barely projecting branch in the water. Then she realized it was moving. She looked more closely and her eyes widened. Hastily she pulled up her feet, tucked them under her and spoke aloud.

"Ohhhh, it's an alligator!"

That's exactly what it was and, though it was only a small one, under three feet long, Lara felt her heart pounding. She imagined that there was a much larger one just under the surface and the thought frightened her. She was considering returning to the house when the sound of the outboard motor touched her ears and the boat carrying William and Barnaby came back into view.

Barnaby was babbling excitedly even before the boat coasted to a stop against the dock with a slight bump.

"It's wonderful back there, Lara! All sorts of birds and animals and turtles and other things. We went into a secret passage that Uncle Danny discovered. You have to see it! We went in only a little way, but it was terrific!"

Lara was eager to see it. "Will you take me out there, too, William? Please?"

"Not today," her cousin answered, tying the boat snugly to the dock. "It's too late. We'll all go out again tomorrow when we have more time."

Lara waited to hear more but the boys remained silent. "Well," she said, "Aren't you going to tell me about it? What did you see?"

William shook his head and it was Barnaby who answered in a rather smug and superior manner. "You'll see."

"Ohhh!" Lara stamped her foot as if she were angry, though she really wasn't. "That's not fair."

Barnaby looked at William. "Can't I just tell her about your big brown bird?"

"Big brown bird?" Lara echoed.

"No!" William shot a sharp look at Barnaby. "She'll find out soon enough."

The rest of the late afternoon and evening passed slowly for Lara. Though she asked her brother and cousin several times more about what they had seen and what kind of bird the big brown bird was, they simply shook their heads and said, "You'll see . . . tomorrow." It was all very frustrating for the little girl.

Lara's brain was so filled with images of the secret passage that she had a difficult time falling asleep. When at last she did drop off, she dreamed about alligators and hungry fish and William's big brown bird, which swooped down and picked her up in its beak. Twice she woke gasping with fear.

In the morning she awakened at Auntie Alice's call from downstairs that breakfast was nearly ready and she quickly hopped out of bed. Some of her fright remained from the nightmare, but she put it aside, fearing that if she mentioned it, Barnaby and William would use it as an excuse not to take her along with them today. She quickly put on the new denim blouse and coveralls Mother had bought her to wear down here. Lara especially liked the coveralls, which had a large bib pocket containing a little gold compact attached to the fabric by a scarlet cord. (It wasn't real gold, of course, since little girls almost never get things made out of real gold, but it definitely *looked* like gold. Actually, it was all plastic.) Lara felt very grown up to have a compact that looked very much like Mother's.

The compact had two compartments: in one there was a receptacle for face powder, a small powderpuff and, on the hinged circular lid, a mirror. In the other there was a miniature frame with space for a picture behind the glass. There had been a picture of Minnie Mouse in it when she first got it, but Lara thought that was childish and now it had been replaced by a picture of Mother that Lara had asked to have. It was an old picture, when Mother was not many years older than Lara — certainly not more than eighteen — and they had laughed together at how closely Lara resembled her mother in the picture, despite the difference in their ages.

Slipping her feet into comfortable tennis shoes, which William had said they all had to wear in the boat, she went downstairs and took her place at the table, where

15

Uncle Danny, William and Barnaby were already seated. Auntie Alice was just coming to the table with a platter of pancakes and sausage links she had prepared and everyone said "ummm" as they tasted how delicious they were.

Lara smiled at Auntie Alice as they ate, feeling a strong attachment for her, even though they'd met for the first time only the day before yesterday. She was warm and soft and every bit as loving as Mother; and Uncle Danny, who looked very much like Father, was so big he was sort of scary at first. Auntie Alice was short and round and smelled like carnations and fresh bread and Fels Naptha soap. Lara and Barnaby agreed that when she hugged them she felt like a big warm pillow. The twins had come here from Chicago for a month's vacation and were met at the airport. Uncle Danny had picked them both up together, one in each arm, and it was almost like going up in an elevator. When he had kissed them in turn, his cheek against theirs was prickly-friendly and his deep chuckle seemed to start rumbling from way down near his shoes, like a big cat purring. He and Father were brothers and once in a while it would come to Lara with a little jolt that Father was not their real father; he had adopted Barnaby and Lara when they were only two, when he married Mother. She told them that their real father, whom they never really knew, had died not long after they were born. To them, their adopted father was just Father and they loved him (and he loved them) every bit as much as if he was really their father. And Uncle Danny was just like him.

As soon as they finished breakfast, Auntie Alice made a lunch for the children to take along in the boat. There were peanut butter sandwiches and oranges and cookies and a tightly capped jar of apple juice, along with three plastic cups. All these she placed in a small Igloo cooler with ice cubes in the bottom to keep them cold. Barnaby noticed that Uncle Danny raised an eyebrow slightly when William told him they were going to Loser's Creek.

"Well," the big man said, "you be careful and stay in the main passage. And don't be gone too long."

His son nodded. "All right, Dad."

Less than ten minutes later they pulled away from the dock, William at the rear operating the motor and the twins side by side in the middle seat. Barnaby's slingshot stuck up out of his back pocket and one of his front pockets bulged with the marbles that were his "ammo."

"What's Loser's Creek and why do you call it that?" Lara asked William when they were well on their way.

"That's what my dad named it," he replied. "There were a lot of overhanging branches he had to cut to open the passage. It took him seven months of sawing and chopping to get it open enough to run the boat through it and he lost a pair of glasses and two machetes while he was doing it. So, when he finished, he named it Loser's Creek."

Because it was hard to talk over the noise of the motor when they were running fast, they didn't speak much after that until they had left the clearer, blue-green open waters and reached the little, hidden dark-water bay. Again there were many egrets and herons and anhingas. The egrets and herons flew off squawking at the intrusion and two anhingas dropped from their perches on mangrove branches into the water and disappeared beneath the dark surface.

"They swim underwater as well as they fly, Lara," William explained. "That's where they catch the food they eat. Little fish."

Lara nodded, not wanting to speak, afraid her voice would quaver. The journey to this bay through the twisting and ever-narrowing waterways had frightened her more than she cared to admit. Only the eager confidence of her brother and cousin provided any degree of assurance for her. She had to keep reminding herself that the boys had been here yesterday and so there was really nothing to worry about. Was there?

Slowly, carefully, William eased the boat toward the center of that crescent indentation of the mangrove shoreline where it looked as if a huge bite had been taken out of it.

"Do what I do now," Barnaby told her. "We have

to duck down in the bottom of the boat for the first twenty or thirty yards. None of the first part's been cut."

"That's so no one else finds this entry into Loser's Creek," William explained. "If other people knew about it, pretty soon it would be all cluttered up with empty cans and sandwich wrappers and other junk. Dad says he wants to keep it pristine. That means unspoiled."

Under William's careful guidance, the prow of the boat nudged into the overhanging branches, bent some of them away and slid through. There was a faint screeching and swishing of twigs and leaves scraping along the sides of the boat and the children concentrated on staying out of the way. Lara felt branches brush across her back as she first bent over and then kneeled in the bottom of the boat to escape them. A number of the oval-shaped, unusually thick mangrove leaves dislodged from the limbs and fell around them. The deeper

inside they went, the dimmer the light became and she suddenly wished very much that she hadn't come.

Behind Lara and Barnaby, William maneuvered the boat slowly and skillfully. He, too, was crouched as low as he could get but soon he began to straighten.

"It's okay," he whispered. "You can sit up now. Just watch out for any low branches still sticking out and duck around them. We're inside now."

Barnaby and Lara resumed their seats and looked about them. It was much brighter now, with cheery speckles of sunlight filtering through the canopy of leaves about five feet above them, turning everything bright green and gold. They were on a long, narrow waterway perhaps four feet wider than the boat. A sort of passageway had been carved through the branches of the mangroves. They could see only about fifty yards ahead, to where the creek went around a sharp bend.

Barnaby pointed toward the bend and put his head close to Lara's and whispered to her. "Right up there, Lara — that's where William's big brown bird stays."

Lara nodded but still did not trust herself to speak. The waterway was so narrow she did not see how William could turn the boat around to get them out. Her heart was beating very fast.

"No talking!" William's command came as a whispered hiss and the only sound after that was the muted putting of the motor at idle speed, moving the boat along quite slowly. Just as they reached the bend and William started making the turn, he cut off the motor and they drifted silently forward.

The bend was almost L-shaped and around the corner there was something that caught the immediate attention of the children. Their three sets of eyes fastened on a thick branch stretched across the passage only a dozen yards ahead. Beyond the branch, the passageway became very dimly lighted, but the branch itself was clearly visible. No more than four feet above the creek, it was draped with ghostly streamers of gray-green Spanish moss trailing nearly to the water surface. On the middle of the limb, facing them, sat a creature staring at them with huge, unblinking eyes. Lara uttered a soft, involuntary gasp.

It was William's big brown bird.

"See!" Barnaby whispered excitedly, his lips close to his sister's ear. "Just like I told you."

Lara's own lips hardly moved as she whispered back. "What is it, Barnaby?"

"Why, silly, it's an owl."

"But it's so *big!*"

Lara had once before seen an owl, but it had been reddish and small — not much larger than a robin — and had tufts on its head, like ears. This bird staring at them with enormous deep brown eyes was over two feet high and very plump and it had no ear-tufts. Its feathers, arranged in vertical lines of light and dark, made it look like a fat little man in a brown pinstripe suit.

"It's a barred owl," Barnaby whispered back, pleased at being able to identify it correctly. Even William had not known what kind of owl it was.

"Hello, Owl," William said aloud. "I'm back again. I brought my cousins."

The big bird sat more erect and tilted its head down toward them slightly to see them better as they drifted closer. The large curved beak opened once and closed with a snap so loud it sounded like a twig breaking. Then the owl turned around and in the same movement leaped off the perch away from them. Spreading huge rounded wings, it swept down within inches of the water and flew in total silence into the deepening dark of the passage ahead. When almost out of sight of them, its flight curved upward and it settled on another branch spanning the creek.

"It's always here," William said, speaking normally now. "Every time I've come, including yesterday with Barnaby, it's been here. Always on the same perch and always flying ahead of the boat from perch to perch. It'll fly again as soon as we get close."

"Oh my," Lara said in a tiny voice. "You mean we're going in *farther?*"

"Sure," William replied. "You'll like it. There's nothing to be afraid of. Trust me. It's really neat."

He pulled the cord and the motor coughed to life with a little sputter and once more the boat moved slowly forward. The three children ducked down to pass beneath the branch that William's big brown bird had been sitting upon and immediately the dimness closed over them and everything around them changed.

3

The Dark Green Tunnel

SUDDENLY the passage became very dimly lighted. The mangrove trees on either side were much more dense and their branches interwoven overhead cut off almost all the sunlight so that everything had become a deep somber green. The gnarled roots of the mangroves that twisted down into the water had been distinctly reddish in the sunlight, but now they had become dark spidery ropes. The water, too, had become much darker, almost black, and looked dangerous to Lara. Misreading her thoughts, William spoke up.

"The water's not dirty. It's just dark because it's stained from the mangrove roots."

"I didn't think it was dirty, William," Lara replied. "I was just thinking about how much darker it is here than earlier . . . and what might be in it."

"Stained with a stuff called tannin," Barnaby put in, remembering having read about it in the library, "just like it was back farther, but now with no sunlight on it, it looks even darker."

Knowing what caused it to be dark did not make Lara any more comfortable. She imagined strange fearsome creatures lurking beneath the surface and she moved closer to the center of the seat and against her brother.

Barnaby felt her tremble and he became concerned. He put an arm around her and spoke reassuringly. "Don't be afraid, Lara. It's okay. Different, that's all."

It was definitely different. The opening Uncle Danny had cut through here was no more than a few inches wider than the boat and the canopy of branches was now much lower — just over their heads. As far ahead as they could see, the passage had become a dark green tunnel.

"Look, Lara," William said, "those are soldier crabs on the roots."

Her gaze followed his pointing finger and she saw them. There were hundreds of small dull black crabs about the size of walnuts. They clung to the roots just above the water and moved about slowly or in little scurrying sideways runs. Now and then they would pause and look toward the passing boat, their eyes projected above their bodies on little stalks.

Lara shuddered, unconsciously pressing even closer to her brother. She thought they looked like nothing so much as horrible big black spiders. She looked behind her at William, who was grinning, and she suddenly knew he had known they would frighten her. It took quite an effort on her part, but she straightened and moved a little away from Barnaby, looking at the crabs more closely.

"How interesting," she said. She glanced again at William and saw his grin had faded and she felt a little surge of triumph.

"We're coming up on the owl again," William announced.

A hundred feet ahead the big brown bird was perched with its back toward them. As they neared, the owl's head slowly swiveled around until it was staring directly over its back at them. Lara felt it was staring directly at her and this made her very nervous. When they were only twenty feet away, one of the owl's eyes slowly closed, as if in an exaggerated wink. Then it popped open, the head snapped back to its original position and once again the owl launched itself from its perch.

As before, it flew low over the water, away from them, quickly becoming no more than a silently moving shadow. It disappeared around another bend.

"That is the strangest bird I have ever seen," Lara said, keeping her voice light. "I'm glad I got a chance to see it. Thank you ever so much, William. Now I suppose we will leave?" She tried to keep the eagerness for this out of her voice.

"Oh, no, not yet," William said. "For one thing, how would we turn around? Dad opened this up all the way to a little hidden lake about a mile ahead. That's where we'll stop and eat lunch before turning around and coming back."

Barnaby nodded. "You'll like it, Lara. You really will."

Lara said nothing but she wished people would quit telling her she would like things. The boys had told her she would like the passage, but she most definitely didn't.

"It's sunny and bright there," Barnaby continued. "There are all kinds of birds and animals and wild orchids blooming and lots of beautiful butterflies. It's a perfect place for a picnic in the boat. You'll really like it."

"All right," Lara said. Her attempt at a smile was not too successful but the boys didn't seem to notice.

They continued foward, the dark green tunnel twisting and turning more and more as they progressed. Here and there they came to wider places where, with care, it would have been possible to turn the boat around, but William passed them by.

The owl had continued ahead of them, flying each time they approached closely but quickly perching again. Every time they neared it, Lara had the eerie feeling the bird was staring at her in particular, but she didn't mention it to her brother and cousin for fear they would think she was being silly and make fun of her. Lara hated being made fun of.

Then something happened to make Lara suddenly feel she hadn't been imagining things where the owl was concerned. The big brown bird landed on a looping vine, which hung like a dark gray clothesline across one of those wider places in the creek. This time as they approached, it suddenly spread its wings but did not take off. The unstable vine swung back and forth precariously with the bird's movement.

William was so surprised that he cut off the motor and the boat slid quietly forward until it came to a stop only ten feet away.

"It's trying to keep its balance," William said.

"It's pretending to be a tightrope walker," Barnaby said.

"It's telling us to stop here," Lara said.

"That's very silly!" There was contempt in William's voice.

"Maybe not," Barnaby put in quickly, coming to her defense but not too sure that William wasn't right.

Lara wasn't listening to them. She was staring at the bird who was staring at her. Quite suddenly all the fear she had been experiencing was gone, even though the huge bird did look rather menacing.

"Maybe it's mad because we followed it so closely," Barnaby continued.

"That's even sillier!" his cousin replied.

The bird opened and closed its beak a number of times

and a succession of snapping sounds filled the heavy air.

"I think it's warning us," Barnaby said, his brow wrinkling in a frown.

"Sillier yet!" William responded with a snort, his mind seeming to have stuck on the concept of silliness.

"Maybe it's going to attack us," Barnaby went on, ignoring William's scorn. "Maybe I'd better shoot it." Even though he had never shot at a living creature before, he reached for the slingshot in his hip pocket.

"No!"

The single word from his twin made Barnaby stop. He looked at her, but she was still staring at the owl and he followed her gaze.

While the bird's fragile perch continued to sway back and forth, the big brown owl slowly closed one wing. The other remained outstretched and the longest pinions were pointing almost like fingers. Lara looked in that direction and so she was first to see what had escaped their attention until now. The deep dark green of the mangrove leaves had an even deeper darkness behind them.

"Start the motor, William," she said quietly. She pointed. "Move us in there."

"In where?" William asked, not yet seeing what she had seen.

"There."

The older boy glanced at the dense screen of mangrove leaves and shook his head. "That's dumb, Lara. There's nothing there. Nothing. We'll just run into the branches."

"Do it, William. *Please!*"

There was a quality in her voice that silenced him and he only nodded grimly. A tug on the cord started the motor and he eased the bow of the boat toward where she was still pointing. His mouth dropped open when, instead of encountering springy branches to hold them back, the boat slid neatly through the curtain of leaves and into the darkness beyond.

4

Four Strange Things

HOWEVER DIM it had been before, now there was nothing but total blackness ahead. As the rear of the boat slid inside, darkness closed behind it as if a heavy velvet curtain had been dropped.

"I don't know about this." Barnaby's small voice in the darkness carried a distinct note of fear.

"We'd better back out of here," said William's voice.

"No," said Lara. The word was spoken in an oddly commanding tone, as was what she said next. "Keep going. At least for a little while."

Their only contact with reality was the feel of the boat beneath them, the soft putt-putting of the motor and the gentle brushing of leaves against them as they passed.

"I'm going to put it in reverse," William announced suddenly, his voice high-pitched with apprehension. "Dad said I shouldn't leave the main passage. I'm going to back us out of here. This is weird."

"Good idea," chimed in Barnaby.

"Wait," said Lara. "There's something ahead. A sort of light. Keep going. It's not far."

William did not answer, but the sound of the motor remained constant and their direction did not change. A faint greenish glow far ahead of them in the darkness gradually brightened as they approached. It was like a speckled curtain at first, but very soon became the light of day seeping through a heavy screen of leaves.

In a few moments William gently nudged the bow of the boat against the dense leaves, pushing them aside, and they slid through easily. With startling suddenness they were out of the darkness and in open water. The wall of foliage closed behind them as if it had never been disturbed. The owl was nowhere to be seen, evidently not having followed them.

Four strange things were immediately apparent.

"Oh, wow," Barnaby murmured, "look at the sun. It's not bright yellow anymore."

The sun was shining brightly, but it now had a distinctly greenish cast rather than yellow.

"And look at the sky," William put in. "It's not blue like it should be."

That was true, too. The green quality of the daylight had not been the result of its being filtered through the leaves. The sky itself was pale green.

The third strange thing was only a little less obvious and it was Lara who noticed it. They were in a large almost circular pool of dark water. The foliage lining the shores was so dense that there would have been no possibility of shoving through. She pointed toward the water.

"Look!" she exclaimed. "There are no reflections." She was absolutely correct. The trees rising from the water's edge did not reflect at all. She leaned over and looked down into the water through which they were slowly moving. There was no reflection there, either. It was like trying to see her own image in a blackboard.

"Most peculiar," Barnaby said. He dipped his hand in the water and though he could see it clearly enough beneath the surface, there was no reflection of his arm or his face looking down or even the side of the boat. "Most peculiar," he repeated.

Directly across the pool from where they had emerged was a very tiny beach. The sand was pale green and it sloped up from the dark water's edge in a narrowing wedge, its margins walled with the same impenetrable growth of mangrove. The fourth strange thing was something in the exact center of that sand and they all saw it simultaneously.

"Wow!" exclaimed Barnaby.

"I don't believe it!" exclaimed William.

"Oh my goodness!" exclaimed Lara.

It was a turnstile.

As they neared the shore William turned off the motor

and the bow of the boat slid neatly up on the sand with a crunchy sound. Immediately Lara leaped out into the soft warm sand. With a little less enthusiasm, Barnaby and William followed. As a good boatsman should, William looked around for a place to tie the line attached to the bow of his boat. Finding nothing suitable, he tugged on the line and wedged the boat more firmly. Then he followed the twins to where they had stopped a few feet away from the turnstile, which was painted green.

"It's a lot like the turnstiles for the subway," Barnaby said.

It was indeed. Just an ordinary turnstile with four arms on top, like a big four-bladed fan pointed upward. It stood on a four-sided metal pedestal that flared out at the bottom and had claw-and-ball feet like an antique bathtub. On the side facing the water (which was the side they were standing on) there were two signs, one above the other. They were white and the top one had one word in large black letters.

ENTRANCE

The other had red letters and said:

DANGER: High Voltage

With wondering looks at one another they walked all the way around the turnstile. On the left- and right-

hand sides there was nothing, but on the side opposite the two signs there were two others. The bottom one was the same as that on the other side, but the top one said:

EXIT

"Entrance and exit to what?" asked William in a grumpy way. He was angry but he didn't know why, not realizing that anger often grows out of fear. "It's just standing out here in the middle of the sand. It doesn't *go* anywhere."

"We don't know that for sure," Lara pointed out. She pointed at the entrance sign. "Let's try it and see."

"I don't think that's a good idea," Barnaby said warily. "See that warning sign? We might get an electric shock."

"Probably only if we have something made out of metal in our pockets," William responded, but he didn't sound very sure of himself.

"All I have is a handkerchief and my compact," Lara said, "and they're not metal at all. And we're all wearing tennis shoes with rubber soles. I think it would be all right."

"My slingshot's just wood and rubber," Barnaby put in. "And my ammo is just marbles."

"Well, I don't have anything metal, either," William said. He sniffed loudly. "But if you think I'm going to touch that thing, you're wrong."

"I'll be the guinea pig," Lara boldly announced. She stepped toward the turnstile.

"No, Lara, don't!" William cried.

It was too late. She reached out and put one finger on an arm of the turnstile. Nothing happened and she smiled at them.

"See, I told you it would be all right."

So saying, she pushed against the arm with both hands. The turnstile creaked and turned, *clickity-clickity*, a quarter-turn in a clockwise manner, allowing her to pass. What happened then was a big shock, but not the kind of shock Barnaby had anticipated.

Lara disappeared.

One moment she was pushing the turnstile arm and moving with it and the next moment, as she lifted her hands from the arm, she was gone.

Barnaby's eyes widened and his face became very pale and his mouth opened in a big O but no sound came out.

"Lara! *Lara!*" William shouted, but there was no answer.

Both of the boys stood rooted in place, not knowing what to do and very frightened. Barnaby's vision began to swim from the tears that flooded his eyes and he echoed his cousin's cry.

"Lara! Where are you? Can you hear me? Lara!"

There was silence for a moment and there's no telling what they would have done next, because almost instantly the turnstile creaked and turned, *clickity-clickity*, but this time in a counterclockwise direction. It stopped when a quarter-turn was completed and just as abruptly as Lara had vanished, she reappeared. Her hands were still in front of her from having pushed the turnstile arm.

"*There* you are," she said, smiling sweetly. "How come you disappeared?"

For an instant they were speechless, but then William found his voice. "Where did you go?" he demanded. "You scared us. What if you hadn't been able to come back?"

She tossed her head. "Oh, William, you worry too much. The signs said entrance and exit, didn't they? Well, I entered and looked around for a little while and then came right back through the exit. I certainly wasn't gone for more than ten minutes and didn't get half enough of a chance to see what —"

"Ten minutes?" Barnaby interrupted. "What are you talking about, Lara? You weren't gone for more than a few seconds."

She was sure he was joking, but then she saw that he was very serious and she frowned. "How very odd," she murmured.

"Never mind that," William said impatiently. "What did you see, Lara?"

"Oh, you should see it!" She clapped her hands together under her chin. "It was just wonderful! There are beautiful grassy hills and big trees and a long narrow lake and, in the distance beyond that, some huge gray mountains!"

"Bull!" William said impolitely. "There are no hills in south Florida to say nothing of mountains."

"But there are," Lara insisted. "Really. If you don't believe it, come with me and see." She turned back toward the turnstile, but stopped and faced them when William said, "Wait!"

Her cousin nodded. "Okay, I have to admit I'm very curious —"

"Me, too!" chimed in Barnaby.

"— and we'll go with you," William continued. "But since we may be gone for a while, we'd better take our lunch with us."

"It won't be much fun carrying that cooler around,"

Barnaby said. He figured that he would be the one who got stuck with carrying it, since he was the younger boy.

"That's true," William admitted, thinking he would probably have to carry it, since he was oldest and strongest.

Lara nodded, knowing she would have to carry it because she was the only girl and boys always made girls do the jobs the boys themselves didn't want to do. "I know!" she said. "Why don't we just have our picnic here on the sand? Then we can go through the turnstile and look around without having to carry anything."

They all agreed that was a marvelous idea and so that's just what they did. They got the cooler out of the boat and spread a big beach towel on the sand and sat there munching deliciously gummy peanut butter sandwiches and crunchy cookies and sipping tangy apple juice from their cups. They left their oranges in the cooler, to have on the way home.

While they were eating, Barnaby and William tried to coax Lara into telling them more about what she had seen when she went through the turnstile, but she only smiled and shook her head.

"You'll see for yourself soon enough," she said mysteriously.

5

Crobbity

"WELL, are you ready?" Lara asked them.

"Sure," replied William, although now he didn't sound quite so sure.

"I guess so," replied Barnaby, his uncertainty evident.

"Then what are you waiting for?" she said. "Push your way through."

"Uhhh, ladies first," William said, giving her a sort of sickly smile.

"Right," Barnaby agreed. "Ladies first."

They were unsuccessful in masking their fear and Lara couldn't keep the mild scorn out of her voice. "You boys are so brave! All right, if that's the way you want it."

She moved past them and shoved the arm of the turnstile with her hands. *Clickity-clickity*. She was gone.

The boys looked at each other and William let the

tip of his tongue pass over lips that had suddenly gone dry. "Maybe only girls can get through," he said. When there was no response from his cousin, he added: "You're next."

Barnaby frowned. "Why me?"

William thought a moment and then brightened. "If anything goes wrong, someone'll have to go for help. You don't know how to operate the boat and even if you did, you wouldn't be able to find your way back."

"But —"

"Don't argue! Go on."

Barnaby swallowed audibly and then thrust against a turnstile arm. *Clickity-clickity.* He disappeared.

By himself now, William groaned. His palms were moist and his knees felt weak. He wished he had not agreed to go and even considered running back to the boat and getting out of here. A wash of shame flooded him and he knew he couldn't do that. He had no choice except to join his cousins, but wished he had a suit of armor and a weapon as protection against whatever they might encounter. Taking a deep breath, he pushed against a turnstile arm.

Clickity-clickity.

"Owww!" he cried. "Owwwwwww!"

He danced about crazily, swatting at the outside of his upper leg. The twins were close by, staring at him openmouthed, not knowing what was wrong or what to do.

There was the smell of smoldering cloth in the air and William continued hopping about making noises of pain. At last there was a tiny thumpy sound as a large coin fell out of his pantleg, bounded off his shoe and landed on some dry leaves. Immediately a little curl of smoke arose as the leaves upon which the coin came to rest turned brown and curled. They didn't catch on fire but for a moment it appeared they would. Evidently one of the leaves was a little damp because there was a faint hissing and a little puff of steam. The hissing faded away quickly and the smoke and steam dissipated.

"Good grief, William!" Barnaby said. "What happened?"

"I forgot I had my lucky silver dollar in my pocket," William gasped, rubbing his leg. He pulled his pocket inside out and there was a browned hole where the coin had burned through. His continued swatting and rubbing had extinguished the smoldering cloth after the coin had fallen free.

Lara was instantly solicitous. "Are you hurt badly? Can we help?"

William shook his head. The momentary pain, more startling than truly damaging, had passed. "No, it's all right now. It just stung at first. Maybe I'll get a blister." He grinned suddenly. "Well, that was some experience."

Barnaby nodded sympathetically, glancing at the silver dollar now lying innocently at their feet. "You can be glad you weren't dressed up in armor. You would have been roasted!"

Remembering his wish moments before stepping through the turnstile, William agreed, breathing a deep sigh of relief. He stooped and touched the coin hesitantly, testing. It was still faintly warm but he could handle it, so he picked it up and showed it to them. His father had given it to him on his birthday last winter and he had carried it with him ever since as a lucky piece. It was an 1859 silver dollar with the picture of a seated woman — Liberty — on one side and an eagle on the other.

"I managed to bring it in," he said, "but I don't think I'll try to take it out. I will take it along while we're here, though, in case we might need it." He dropped it into the opposite front pocket of his pants. "Just don't let me forget and go back through the exit with it when we leave."

The children turned their attention to the surroundings. Behind them was the turnstile, its top sign now reading *EXIT*. The rest was as Lara had so briefly described it. They were on the rounded top of one of many rolling hills covered with lush dark green grasses. Large shade trees with enormous gnarled trunks, thick branches and great domes of lavender-green foliage were here and there on the knolls, singly or in small groups. Well below them, close to the long narrow lake, the land was heavily forested. The water in the lake was a very pale green. Far in the distance beyond, forbidding gray mountain peaks jutted upward like jagged fangs.

William forgot his momentary pain as they looked about them. His eyes widened and his mouth opened in wonderment.

"This doesn't look like the Everglades," he muttered.

"Isn't it pretty!" Lara exclaimed. She pointed to a dense grove of trees close to them. "Those trees! I've never seen anything like them."

"And the lake," Barnaby said, just as excitedly. "It's so calm and green! Why, it looks like fine grass — like a huge green on a golf course."

"Let's explore!" Lara cried suddenly, clapping her hands together.

"Good idea," agreed Barnaby, who wished he'd thought of that.

"I don't know," William said slowly. "Suppose we got lost. We'd never get home again."

"No problem," Lara said with assurance. "All we have to do is locate some special landmark close to here and then we can always find it again."

They all peered around again, more keenly this time, because now they used the eyes of pathfinders instead of tourists.

"There's a big rock," Barnaby pointed out.

They looked where he pointed and sure enough, well down the slope and partially hidden by one especially large tree in the grove was a very large flat-topped rock sticking out of the grass. At once they began walking toward it, with William taking the lead and his cousins side by side behind him. Lara had a hard time keeping up because her legs were very short and one of William's steps equaled two of hers.

As they walked, they looked back occasionally to keep track of the turnstile, which was very easy to see because it was the only object on top of this particular knoll. At first it was easy walking because the ankle-deep grass grew from very smooth ground and they were moving downhill. But as they came closer to the rock the grass was less luxuriant and the ground uneven and stony. The children had to pay attention to where they were walking to keep from twisting their ankles and so they didn't look back until they reached the base of the rock. They stopped and inspected it, finding it to be considerably higher than their heads. William reached out and put his palm against its smooth side. He nodded and spoke seriously.

"You were right, Barnaby," he said. "It *is* a big rock."

By big, he meant it was much bigger than a truck, say, but certainly not as big as a large house. Somewhere in between would be exactly what he meant.

It was Barnaby who also discovered, in the next breath,

that they could no longer see the turnstile. This was a little worrisome to them all.

"Why don't we walk around it," Lara suggested, "and see if there is some way we can climb to the top? Maybe from up there we could see the turnstile."

She led the way and they found the sides were much too steep and smooth to climb. A huge branch from the nearest tree overhung the rock, only a foot from its top surface, but the trunk of the tree was so large and the bark so smooth that there would be no way to climb it. They continued following the base of the rock. When they were almost back to the point where they had begun their circumnavigation, someone spoke.

"Crobbity."

Lara stopped so suddenly that William nearly ran into her and Barnaby almost ran into him. She looked at her cousin.

"Did you say crobbity?"

"No." He shook his head and turned to Barnaby. "Did you say crobbity?"

"How could I say crobbity?" Barnaby said. "I don't even *know* the word crobbity. What does it mean?"

"It means hello," said a voice. "Hello, hello, hello. It also wishes you health and happiness and good fortune. Then, too, it means I am friendly. It also asks if you are friendly. In a more definitive way, it extends the hope that the journey which brought you here was pleasant and that if you are willing to trust me, I am willing to trust you."

The words came in quite a rush and, since the voice was above them, all three of the children looked up. A very small man was sitting on the broad branch overhanging the top of the rock, his legs dangling. At first he appeared to have a ring of red fur framing his face. A closer look proved it to be an extraordinarily long red moustache whose ends had been loosely twisted on each side and brought up to the top of his bald head. There they had been tied together in a very fancy bow resembling a butterfly. His face was very craggy, with large dark eyes set wide apart over a remarkably small round nose. His ears were tiny and he had almost no chin, but his mouth was extremely wide. He wore a dark green vest and very baggy knickers of the same color. Socks of alternating narrow bands of green and white covered his thin lower legs and disappeared into somewhat clumsy-looking square shoes. Around his neck he wore a wide band of what appeared to be dull metal strands.

"Of course," he continued, speaking without pause, "in its most esoteric form, the word crobbity is also a birthday greeting, anniversary wish and a declaration of thanksgiving for honoring me with your presence."

"That's an awful lot of meaning for just one word of greeting," William said.

"It must be hard for the person you're talking to to know what you mean," said Barnaby.

"Crobbity," said Lara, bowing her head respectfully.

"Ah, that's nice," said the little man, his gaze settling on her. "Nice, nice, nice. You are obviously a person of breeding and consideration. Crobbity."

He looked down at Barnaby and his voice became gruff. "The meaning one infers from the greeting depends on many interlocking factors of expression, delivery and tonal quality. That meaning becomes more implicit the more discerning the listener happens to be. In other words, if you're not a total clod, you know. Crobbity."

He shifted his gaze to William and his voice became even more stern. "Does not your vocabulary include words of salutation with more than one meaning?"

"Well," William said slowly, frowning in thought, "hi means hello. Maybe even how are you."

"How marvelously versatile," the little man said dryly. "Nothing else?"

William brightened as he dredged up a word from memory. "Yes. Yes, indeed. Aloha."

"Aloha?"

"Yes, aloha. It means both hello and goodbye."

"*Opposites?*" the little man said unbelievingly. "How unutterably preposterous. One would never know whether someone was coming or going. Say what you mean or say nothing at all, that's my motto. Yessir, that's my motto. Motto, motto, motto. Say what you mean. Crobbity. Well? I'm waiting."

"Waiting?" William said, confused.

"That's what I said," the little man snapped. "Waiting. Waiting, waiting, waiting!"

William stood there helplessly, not knowing what was expected of him. Lara motioned to her cousin and he leaned down so she could cup his ear and whisper to him. The light of understanding came into his eyes and he looked up at the little man again, who was now standing on the branch and who was clearly only about three feet tall.

"Crobbity," William said, bowing slightly.

The little man rolled his eyes toward Barnaby.

"Crobbity," Barnaby said in a small voice.

"Ah, wonderful!" The little man's gruffness vanished and his unusually wide mouth spread in a grin so broad it seemed almost to separate his head from his neck. "How wonderful, wonderful, wonderful to welcome my dear friends. Dear, dear, dear friends. Well, don't just stand there. Come in!"

"In where, sir?" Lara asked.

"The tree, of course," he answered, tapping the branch upon which he sat. "Where else? The door's on the back side and it's unlocked. Come, come, come!"

The three walked immediately to the tree and circled around to the other side. The door was there, set in an oval frame. It was small enough that they would have to stoop over to enter. Barnaby grasped the handle and tried to push it open, but it wouldn't push. Then he tried to pull it open, but it wouldn't pull.

"I thought he said it was unlocked," he said.

"Try sliding it," Lara suggested.

The door slid smoothly as Barnaby tried this, exposing a dimly lighted interior in which a set of wooden stairs spiraled upward around the inside hollow.

"I don't know about this," William said, becoming wary.

"We could be stepping into trouble," Barnaby said.

"Perhaps," Lara said. "Then again, perhaps not."

They stood there quietly, each waiting for one of the other two to make a decision.

"Well," William said at last, "we'll never know unless we try, right?"

"Right," said Barnaby, nodding.

"I agree," said Lara. "Who'll go first?"

No one spoke for a moment and then William suggested they vote on it. They did so quickly and then in single file they stooped over and entered the portal and started up the stairway. Not unexpectedly, the majority had voted Lara to lead the way.

6

Mr. Beadle

THE SPIRAL STAIRS led the children to a landing where there was an open door leading out onto the big branch. This is where the little man with the red moustache met them. He motioned them to follow and led them up still higher in the huge tree to a very strange circular room. Picking his way carefully through an amazing variety of objects, he led them to where, pleasantly grouped about a low table, there were soft comfortable chairs and a sofa. Here he bowed graciously to Lara and very properly shook hands with the two boys.

"Sit, sit, sit," he bade them. "I'll join you in just a moment and we'll get acquainted."

He moved quickly to a sideboard and began pouring piping-hot peppermint tea into fragile little cups and heaping a serving plate with pastries from a warmer. A bit hesitantly, they sat down and looked about wonderingly as he worked. Lara thought she had never seen a more cluttered room, nor one more fascinating.

Bric-a-brac was everywhere: little carved figurines and pieces of pottery, small framed pictures, interesting fossils and odd mineral specimens, and a whole collection of unusual weapons. A short coat of chain mail hung from a peg near the door and a spike-studded mace hung beside it. The rug was thick, rose-colored wall-to-wall carpeting and there was hardly a place on its surface not taken up with furniture or with baskets, boxes and containers filled with other items. There was a small fireplace and on the center of its mantelpiece was a pottery vase containing a nicely arranged spray of beautiful flowers. Two charming glass lanterns, one at each end of the mantel, shed a surprising amount of light. Built-in bookcases flanking the fireplace were filled with volumes, some of which were obviously very old. On the wall over a small desk were several scenic pictures. There was a little dining table with four small chairs along with an open cupboard well stocked with dishes. Another spiral staircase across the room led up to a closed door.

There was only one window, which was very narrow. It looked out across the rolling hills toward the lake. A shaft of pale green sunlight streamed through, illuminating a bright yellow bird about the size of a very small chicken, which was perched on an uncommonly broad windowsill. The bird was evidently asleep, since its head was tucked under one wing and it was snoring rather loudly.

"Well now," said the little man, setting a tray on the low table before them, "let's refresh ourselves and get acquainted." He placed a cup of tea before each and indicated they should help themselves to the scones, then settled himself with a sigh in one of the chairs. He opened his mouth to speak, but then glanced at the bird in an irritated way.

"Boggle!" he shouted. "Shut up!"

The yellow bird stirred and the snoring stopped, but it kept its head under its wing.

"That's better," the little man said, turning back to the children apologetically. "He's only been with me a short time. Most aggravating employee I've ever had. And boring. By far the most boring."

He picked up his cup and appreciatively sniffed the tendril of vapor rising from it. "Ahhh," he murmured. "Perfect." He slurped it noisily and then set the cup down and began speaking rapidly.

"My name is Beadle," he told them. "As you've no doubt deduced, I am gatekeeper here. A very lonely job, I must say. Yessir, lonely, lonely, lonely. And Boggle's never been one for intelligent conversation. There just aren't many travelers entering Verdancia these days. How wonderful to have visitors again. It's been so long. Let me see . . ." He placed a finger to his chin and his brow furrowed with thought. "Why, it must be all of three hundred years since I've checked anyone through. That's not a record, you understand, but it's a respectable time. Indeed it is. Indeed, indeed, indeed."

"Three hundred years, Mr. Beadle?" William said, picking up his cup.

"Verdancia, Mr. Beadle?" Barnaby said, taking one of the scones.

Mr. Beadle took no notice of their interruptions, but continued speaking as if he were finding nourishment of his own merely in having the opportunity to talk to someone. He talked and talked, engaging in a rambling monologue that gave the children no opportunity whatever to comment or ask questions. He told them about Darkland and Brightland and Green Lake and the Tempest Ocean. As if they knew exactly what he was talking about, he mentioned the Festival of the Satyrs and the Dance of the Fauns. With some sadness he commented on the continuing strife between the Warted Gnomes of Odusp and the Selerdorian Dwarfs. He spoke with some degree of authority about dragons and sea serpents and about the nocturnal Vulpines and the crepuscular Krins. He talked about individuals named Ceepo and Li and Holta Weedie and Figgawoon. His voice became suddenly filled with utmost reverence when he mentioned Mag Namodder and was still heavy with respect when he spoke of Prince Daw of Rubiglen. His face darkened, however, and he unconsciously fingered his woven metal necklace as he whispered fearfully about the harsh rule of the Skull King, Thorkin. Then, without even stopping to take a breath, he shot a question at the children.

"Who are you?"

The abruptness took them off balance. Barnaby couldn't answer because his mouth was filled with a big bite of the scones. William was drinking his peppermint tea, so he couldn't answer either.

"My name is Lara," said Lara. "It's a pleasure to meet you, Mr. Beadle. This is my brother, Barnaby. And this is our cousin, William, whom we've been visiting in Everglades City."

"Everglades City?" said Mr. Beadle. "Hmmm. That's a new one on me. I know it's not in Verdancia and I don't think it's in Mellafar or Rubiglen." His gaze suddenly narrowed with suspicion. "Surely it's not in Twilandia!"

Lara shook her head. "I don't know any of those places, Mr. Beadle. Everglades City is in Florida."

"Which is in the United States," added Barnaby, who had swallowed his mouthful of scones.

"Which is in North America," put in William, setting down his teacup.

"Those are the strangest names I've ever heard," Mr. Beadle said. "Strange, strange, strange. And I have no idea where those places are."

As he slurped the last of his tea, he eyed Lara with a disconcerting intensity over the top of his cup. "You say this one, Barnaby, is your brother?" He glanced at the boy, then back at the girl, who nodded. "I take it he is a year older?"

"No sir." Lara shook her head.

"Younger, then?" Mr. Beadle seemed surprised.

"No sir, not really, except by a few minutes. We are twins."

The little man gasped and dropped his teacup. It bounced off the arm of his chair and thumped to the rose-colored carpet. Fortunately, since it was part of a tea set that had been out of production for years, it did not break. Nevertheless, Mr. Beadle didn't even notice whether it had broken or not.

"*Twins!*" His countenance darkened and he came to his feet. "You must realize, I have no option but to report this at once."

William opened his mouth to speak, but the words died unuttered when Mr. Beadle pointed a finger at him. Lara and Barnaby were watching them, totally befuddled.

"Don't you *dare* try to bribe me!" the little man spluttered, shaking his finger in William's face. He drew himself up proudly. "I am — and always have been! — a loyal government employee. Incorruptible, that's what I am. Pure. And honest. Pure, pure, pure. Besides, you don't look as if you would have enough. How many coins do you have?"

"Why, just one, Mr. Beadle, but —"

"Silence! You dare to come into my very home and try to bribe me to close my eyes to my duty! And with only *one* coin? For shame!"

He spun around and strode toward the window, bawling loudly as he went: "*Boggle!* There's work to do — get ready!"

The yellow bird uncovered his head, blinking. He, too, wore a tiny band of woven metal about his neck. He yawned widely and stretched out his wings to their full length. He did a rapid series of knee-bends with wings still out, then closed them and ran several quick laps around the windowsill. Finally, he looked at Mr. Beadle, who was at the desk with a quill pen in his hand. The little man was writing with furious speed, mouthing the words as he did so, which was something Lara's teacher had told her never to do, no matter whether she was reading or writing.

"I'm ready, Boss," Boggle said. "Boy, am I ready! You'll be amazed at how ready I am. I've never been so ready in my life. Why, I'm so ready —"

"Boggle, shut up!" said Mr. Beadle, looking up briefly and frowning. "You are undoubtedly the most tiresome bird I've ever encountered. Now be quiet till I'm finished here."

"Sure thing, Boss. Quiet's the very thing. I'll be so quiet you won't even know I exist. Mum's the word.

You've never heard anything so quiet as I can be. Not a sound. Not even a chirp or a whist —"

"SILENCE!"

With a hurt expression, Boggle turned and stared out the window, but Lara was sure she could still hear him muttering under his breath. As Mr. Beadle returned to his writing, she motioned to her brother and cousin and the three of them put their heads close together.

"What are we going to do?" she whispered.

Barnaby hunched his shoulders. "I don't know," he whispered back, "but I sure don't like it."

"Me neither," hissed William. "We've been here too long now. We've got to get back home. They'll be getting worried."

"I think we ought to make a run for it," Barnaby continued whispering. "Mr. Beadle's only three feet tall. We could outrun him easily. The door's still open downstairs. All we have to do is get outside and run up the hill. Once we're through the turnstile, we're safe."

"But what if he follows us through?" Lara said. She was fighting hard to keep from crying.

"I don't think he can, Lara," William said. "Didn't you see that big wide woven metal necklace he wears? He'd fry with that on."

"I agree," Barnaby agreed.

"I guess we can try," Lara said, though somewhat dubiously.

"Get ready then," William said, taking command. "When I say three, we run. One . . . two . . . three!"

They leaped from their seats and rushed to the steps, then clattered down them as fast as they could go. Behind them they heard Boggle squawk loudly.

"Boss! They're escaping! They're running away, Boss! Boy, look at them go down those stairs! They're escaping, Boss! Now that's what I call taking it on the lam! Listen to that racket they're making on the stairs! They're getting away! Did you ever see such an escape? They're almost outside, Boss. Listen to them go! They're really escaping, Boss. They're going out the door now and —"

"Will you shut up!" Mr. Beadle's voice came to them just as the three plunged out of the door and started up the knoll as fast as they could run, which wasn't all that fast because the loose rocks kept turning under their feet, causing them to stumble. William glanced back and was just in time to see the little man emerge from the first landing door and run out onto the big branch over the rock.

"Stop!" he shouted at them.

Of course, they didn't.

"I warned you," he called again. He raised his arm and pointed toward them. "*Ossyfia!*" he cried loudly.

A tiny ball of intense green light formed on the tip of his index finger, poised there a moment and then disengaged itself and moved toward the fleeing children. Its speed and size increased as it arrowed toward them. Before they had run ten more steps, it overtook them, enveloping them in bright green glare.

The burst of light about them lasted only a second but instantly they were paralyzed, all three of them, from the neck down. Lara was stopped in a position of full run, the heel of her left foot and toe of her right still on the ground. Barnaby, arms outstretched, was frozen in a half crouch, having just been in the act of rising from a stumble. William had stiffened in an approximation of the statue of Mercury, messenger of the gods, with one foot on the ground and the other stretched far out behind him.

"Oh oh," Barnaby panted, "I think we're in trouble."

William didn't say anything and Lara couldn't, because she was crying too hard to talk. Since they could still turn their heads, they looked back and saw Mr. Beadle disappearing into the tree. In a few moments he emerged from the lower door, carrying a folded piece of paper in one hand and, in the other, a mail pouch almost as large as himself. Boggle was riding on his shoulder.

"Dear me," the little man puffed as he came up to them, "this is all very irregular. You should have stopped when I told you to."

"Let us go!" William said angrily. "You have no right to hurt us or hold us prisoner."

"I have not hurt any of you," Mr. Beadle protested. "Nor do I intend to. No, indeed. No, no, no. As for holding you prisoner, that is quite within my province. It clearly states in the regulations section of *The Gatekeeper's Code* — that's Section XII, Number 6, Clause (b) — that the Official Gatekeeper, that's me, is fully authorized to apprehend and detain any person or persons, that's you, guilty of illegally, unlawfully and fraudulently using the turnstile in the Province of Verdancia."

He paused, but before they could reply, he went on. "Were that not enough," he said, staring at William's cousins, "these two are, by their own admission, *twins!*"

Mr. Beadle opened the mouth of the huge mailbag and dropped in the folded piece of paper he still held, which was evidently the message he had been writing. It was also quite obviously the only thing in the bag.

He pulled the drawstrings tight and tied them in a square knot.

"All right, Boggle," he said brusquely. "Get this message to the castle as fast as you can."

"I'll do it fast, Boss," Boggle said cheerily. "Boy, I'll do it so fast you won't believe it. There's never been a message delivered as quickly as this one will be. No sir! I'll carry this one so fast it'll amaze you. Why, Boss, my wings will blur with the speed I'm mak —"

"Oh, shush!" Mr. Beadle broke in wearily. "Just take it and go."

"Mr. Beadle!" Lara said, anger forcing her tears aside. "That poor little bird can't carry that big mailbag. Why don't you just give him the letter to carry by itself?"

The little man shook his head. "Can't do it. Regulations stipulate — Section IV, Number 2, Clause (a) — that all dispatches shall be sent in duly authorized government mail pouches, without exception. Boggle . . . GO!"

"I'm going, Boss," the bird replied, flying off his shoulder and grasping the drawstring of the pouch in his beak. "Boy, am I going! You've never seen anything going like I'm going!" He strained at the load, his wings becoming a buzzing blur in the air, like a hummingbird's. "I'm . . . I'm . . . going," he grunted. "Oh, my, what a load . . . but, I'm going, Boss. I'm really going! Just watch how I'm going. . . . No one's ever gone . . . like I'm . . . going. . . ."

Little by little he gained altitude with the bag and even when he was quite a long distance from them, heading toward Green Lake and the Gray Mountains, his voice drifted back to them.

"Boy, look how I'm going. . . . I'm really going now, Boss."

7

The Centaurs

WHAT FOLLOWED after Boggle left with his message was not very pleasant for the three children. Mr. Beadle shook his head and clucked his tongue sadly, "tsk-tsk-tsk," as he turned around; he continued to do this all the way back to his tree. He disappeared inside and didn't come out again for ever so long.

It was hours before they heard a rumbling sound coming their way and only then did Mr. Beadle emerge and stand near his door looking toward the woods. A short time after that, half a dozen of the strangest creatures the children had ever seen came out of the woods at a brisk trot. Each had the body of a horse but the bare torso and arms of a strong, well-built young man. Each, except the leader, was carrying a dark green shield strapped to one forearm and hand, and a bow and one arrow in the other, along with a quiverful of arrows strung over the shoulder. Each had a large broadsword in a scabbard strapped to his side about where the body of the man merged with the shoulders of the horse. They wore hats made from beautiful iridescent feathers of green and blue. A single large plume sprang from the back of the hat and these single plumes flowed gracefully over their backs. Their hooves made a heavy drumming sound, but more of the noise came from a vehicle directly behind them. It was a large two-wheeled wooden cart drawn by a magnificent stag with enormous antlers. The wheels of the car were also wooden and bumped and thumped over the small rocks on the ground.

"Lara . . . William . . . look!" Barnaby said. "Those are Centaurs! I've seen pictures of them in books."

They were every bit as amazed as he and all three watched as Mr. Beadle ran out to meet them. The Centaurs stopped and Boggle, who had been riding on the back of the leader, dropped his mail pouch to the ground and flew to the little man's shoulder. Their hooves pawing the ground, the Centaurs listened to what Mr. Beadle was saying, though it was too far for the children to hear. However, they saw him turn and point to them. Immediately the Centaurs trotted toward them, the cart following behind and Mr. Beadle running to keep up behind the cart. Boggle, on his shoulder, flapped his wings to keep his balance.

"See here," William began at once when the Centaurs reached them, "we are very late for getting home and there's going to be serious trouble if you don't release us at once." He was both frightened and angry, but the anger was stronger at the moment and it was directed at Mr. Beadle. "Now, you take off this magic spell you've cast on us or whatever it is and let us be on our way."

"Oh my, my, my, no," said the little man, somewhat apologetically. His long red moustache had come untied and its ends were dragging the ground. "I can't do that."

"You must!" William went on, eyes blazing. "It isn't fair. It's cruel and it is no way to treat guests."

"You were only guests while you were in my home," Mr. Beadle replied. "When you so rudely ran off without even saying goodbye, you ceased being guests. But apart from that," he added, "I didn't say I *won't* lift the spell. I said I *can't*. Can't, can't, can't! A reversal spell is not within my purview. The powers bestowed on gatekeepers are very limited." He seemed embarrassed at having to admit this.

"Enough! King Thorkin is waiting and it isn't wise to try his patience." It was the leader of the Centaurs who spoke. He had thick black eyebrows and similar dark hair curled out from beneath his feathered cap. Around his neck was a woven metal necklace not unlike Mr. Beadle's. All the other Centaurs wore them, too. Even the stag had one around his neck.

"Excuse me, Tark." A look of fear crossed the little man's face and he fell silent at once, self-consciously busying himself at retying the moustache over the top of his head. The Centaur named Tark ignored him and leaned down to inspect William, his face only a few inches from the boy's.

"Your name?"

"William."

"Where is your torque?"

William was puzzled. "What is a torque?" he asked.

The Centaur touched the twisted metal band on his own neck. "This is a torque and it is required wearing for everyone in Mesmeria."

"Mesmeria?" Barnaby piped up. "I thought Mr. Beadle said we were in Verdancia."

"Verdancia," said Tark, glancing at the other boy, "is the principal province of the Kingdom of Mesmeria. There are three others — Mellafar, Rubiglen and Selerdor. Mesmeria is also called Brightland, because this is where the sun always shines. On the other side of the world," he continued, almost as if giving a lecture, "beyond the Tempest Ocean, is the continent called Darkland, comprised of the provinces of Odusp, Bluggia and the Great Unknown Lands, which begin at the Chalkyn Desert. Between Brightland and Darkland is a fairly wide area that is neither light nor dark. That area, which stretches all the way around the world, is called Dymzonia and it is inhabited by the fierce crepuscular Krins. I once was on an expedition that fought the Krins. Terrible, just terrible!"

"What about Twilandia?" Barnaby asked.

Instantly Tark stiffened and his eyes narrowed. "What do you know of Twilandia?" he demanded suspiciously.

"Nothing," Barnaby said hurriedly, frightened by the change in the Centaur. "Mr. Beadle mentioned it to us. I was wondering why you didn't say anything about it."

"Twilandia is not to be discussed, *ever!*" Tark growled. "Now let's get back to the matter of your crimes. Here in Verdancia, as in all other Mesmerian provinces, the torque must be worn, according to a royal edict from King Thorkin. It is proof of our fealty to him and a token of his love for us. By wearing it, we exist under his protection. Those who do not wear it are considered to be enemies. The penalty is the same as that for being one of a set of twins — a very severe penalty, I'm afraid."

"How severe?" William asked nervously.

"Death," said Tark, "without exception."

"Oh dear!" It was Lara, speaking for the first time. "Oh dear, that's awful. What kind of king would execute his own people just for not wearing a stupid metal collar, or just for being one of a pair of twins, which is nobody's fault?"

The leader of the Centaurs looked at her closely now, which he hadn't done before. Instantly his eyes widened and he backed up a step or two.

"My Lady!" he gasped. "How can this be? We were

told you were dead and the prophecy false. Is the prophecy true, then, after all?"

Lara was taken aback at a sudden respect he showed her and thoroughly confused by his remarks. "I don't know about any prophecy," she said, "and as you can see, I certainly am not dead. But I *am* very uncomfortable in this position and wish you would release us from the spell Mr. Beadle placed us under."

"Forgive me, My Lady, I cannot," he replied, obviously embarrassed. "I have no spell for doing so. That can come only from King Thorkin or one of his advisers. I will get you back there as quickly as possible. I'm sure the spell will be lifted immediately upon our arrival."

At once he gave an order to the other five Centaurs under his command. The children were lifted carefully and placed side by side in the two-wheeled cart. The boys were loaded first, beginning with William. It was while they were busy with him that Boggle, who had been sitting on Mr. Beadle's shoulder, took to wing and flitted about the group as they worked, alighting here and there. He landed briefly on the cart and hopped onto the top of William's head as they propped him up against the railings on the left side of the cart. From there he flew to the back of one of the Centaurs, where he perched for a moment as the loading of William was going on. Next, he flew to Barnaby and alighted on his arm, cocking his head and looking at the boy in a silly way. When the Centaurs began lifting him, he took off again and landed on Lara's shoulder. He leaned toward her ear and whispered so only she could hear.

"I did not recognize you, My Lady. Please, don't talk. Just listen. Because of the prophecy, you must not go to the castle. If you do, King Thorkin will have the three of you executed. Your only hope is to reach Mag Namodder. I think I can dissolve the spell you're under, but it will take a little while."

Noticing that Mr. Beadle had looked their way, the yellow bird hopped from Lara's shoulder to the top of her head and then down on the other shoulder, as if he were inspecting her. Again, as the little man turned his attention back to the loading of Barnaby, he leaned close to her ear and continued whispering hurriedly.

"When you reach the second forest, called Deep Woods, it becomes very dark. Watch for the giant tree that the path comes close to. On your life, do not move until then. When you reach that point, slip away if you can to the back of the tree. You'll know what to do then. Good luck, My Lady."

Boggle stretched out his wings and leaped from her shoulder. As he did so, he let the outermost feathers of one wing brush lightly across the side of her face. Even as he flew back to perch again on Mr. Beadle's shoulder, Lara felt a warm glow beginning to spread through her from where the feathers had touched her cheek.

By this time Barnaby had been loaded on the right

side of the cart, leaving just enough room for his sister in the middle. The Centaurs came to her and picked her up carefully and moved to the cart with her. Just as they did so, the warmth flooded all through her and she felt her fingers and toes begin to tingle. The sensation was very much like in times past when she had stayed in the wrong position too long and her foot or hand had gone to sleep. It was painful enough that she almost cried out, but she clenched her teeth and managed to keep silent. No one saw the tear that rolled from one eye and dribbled down her cheek.

The urge to move, to stretch her muscles after being in the same position for so long, was very strong, but so was the fear that had risen in her about the danger Boggle had mentioned and his warning that she was not to move. With great effort, she remained in her running position, just as Barnaby and William were in theirs.

Tark gave an order and the big stag strained at its harness and the cart rumbled forward. The other five Centaurs took a position a few yards ahead of the cart. Tark looked down at the little man and dipped his head slightly.

"Say nothing of what has happened here to anyone, Beadle," he said. "You've done well. I will mention you favorably in my report to the King."

Mr. Beadle beamed. "Thank you. I always do my very best. Always, always, always."

Tark wheeled about and galloped away, overtaking

the rumbling cart and taking a position in the lead. As they disappeared into the woods, Boggle leaped into flight from Mr. Beadle's shoulder.

"Boggle!" the little man called. "Where are you going? Get back here."

"In a little while, Boss," the yellow bird's voice drifted back to him. "I'll be back in just a little while. Why, it'll be such a little while you'll hardly know I was gone. I'll be back so fast it'll make your head spin. Not much more than the blink of an eye. You've never seen anyone who'll be back in such a little while as I will, Boss, just you wait and see."

And Boggle, still talking, disappeared over the treetops.

Mr. Beadle stamped his foot. "Dratted bird!" he grumbled as he walked back toward his tree house.

8

The Second Woods

ALTHOUGH aching to move, Lara maintained her position in the cart as it bumped down the hill and into the forest. She was not in a good place for comfort, since every time the cart tilted a little one way or another, she was sandwiched between the boys. Their elbows and shoulders nudged her over and over, as hers did to them, and there was plenty of groaning and grunting. Over the rumbling of the wooden wheels and thudding of hooves, the Centaurs could not hear them. Nor could they hear the whispered conversation that sprang up among the children.

"What are we going to do?" Barnaby said, a definite quavering in his voice.

"I don't know," William answered. "I don't like the sound of this King Thorkin. Didn't Mr. Beadle call him the Skull King? What do you suppose that means?"

"Sounds like he's a real creep," Barnaby ventured.

Then he added, in an attempt at lightness that he didn't really feel, "Maybe he's a walking skeleton." He laughed weakly.

"That's not funny at all, Barnaby," Lara said. "We're in worse trouble than you realize. King Thorkin is going to have us killed."

"Lara!" William said sharply. "That's an awful thing to say. Things are bad enough as they are. This is no time to make up scary stories."

"I'm not making up anything," Lara retorted. "I was told that by Boggle."

"*That* dumb bird!" Barnaby scoffed, not wanting to believe what his twin was saying.

"He isn't dumb at all," Lara said. "That's nothing but an act. He speaks very well when he wants to. He's not only smart, he's got magical powers, too." She lowered her voice so that they had to tilt their heads in her direction to hear. "He removed my spell."

"He did?" the boys exclaimed together.

"Shhhh, not so loud."

In about half an hour they emerged from the woods along the dim trail they had been following, and the bright green sunlight made them squint their eyes. The Centaurs looked back at them and were satisfied all was well. The trail became a road — two wheel-tracks, actually — largely overgrown with grass from disuse. But the ground was smooth and so the Centaurs picked up more speed and the stag broke into a trot to keep his distance behind. At one point, Tark left the others and trotted back to the wagon and around it, looking at them closely. Lara was careful to remain just as stiff as her cousin and brother. Within an hour they approached another forest, much more extensive than the first, and Tark galloped back to his position in front of the party. Immediately the children, who had remained silent all that time, began whispering again.

"Boggle really took your spell away, Lara?" William said in an excited voice. "You can move now?"

"Not completely," she admitted, "but it's coming back. It started in my fingers and toes. Now I'm tingly all over. It hurts, sort of, but I think I could move if I tried."

Barnaby was still skeptical. "Then why are you still standing in that running position?" He sniffed. "I know if I could move, I'd be getting into a more comfortable position. Oh, I'm so stiff!"

"I don't dare let them know I can move," she said. "There's no telling what would happen, but they'd almost surely stop me from escaping."

"Escaping?" William whispered. "You're going to escape?"

"Yes. Boggle told me where to do it and what to do then."

"Where?" Barnaby whispered.

"When?" William whispered. "And what will you do then?"

Lara's lower lip quivered. "In this woods ahead of us," she whispered to her brother, "by a specially big tree." She turned her head to look at her cousin. "And soon, William, but I don't know exactly when. I'll know it when I see that tree. As for what I'll do then," she added, "I don't know for sure, only that somehow I have to find Mag Namodder. Boggle said she's our only hope. He said I'd know what to do when I got behind the tree. Rescuing you two will be the most important thing. But . . . but . . . I don't know how I'll ever be able to do that." She began to cry.

"Don't cry, Lara," Barnaby said quickly. "You'll be just fine, I know it. But just to be sure, you'd better take my slingshot with you. And some ammo."

Barnaby had taught Lara how to shoot with his slingshot and she had learned reasonably well, though she was nowhere near so good with it as he. Now, when she hesitated, he insisted.

"Take it! Don't argue. I can't use it now and you may need it for protection. The ammo's in my front pocket."

Still not too sure about doing so, Lara, maintaining her own stiff posture as much as possible, took the slingshot from his hip pocket and put it into hers. Then she reached into his front pocket and took out a handful of marbles. Since her hand was small, she got only six of them, and these she put into her own front pocket.

"Thank you, Barnaby," she said, "but I still feel you should keep it."

"No," he said, "I'll be all right. And so will you. You'll think of something to do to help us, I know it."

"Sure," put in William. "Maybe you'll be able to find someone who can help." He paused a moment, then swallowed and spoke again. "But, listen, Lara. . . . If you can't find someone here to help, then you'll have to save yourself. Maybe somehow you can get back to the turnstile and go through and bring help from the other side."

Lara nodded, but the same thought was in all three of their minds: Even if Lara *did* get through the turnstile, she didn't know how to start the outboard motor. And even if she got the motor started, she didn't know how to operate the boat. And even if she figured out how to operate the boat, she would have no idea of how to find her way back through the winding passages to Everglades City. Besides, Boggle had told her how urgent it was that she find Mag Namodder.

A pall of gloom settled over them as they entered the larger woods. It was immediately very dim under the trees and grew dimmer the deeper they penetrated, because the trees here were much larger than previously.

The trail twisted about and the air became dank and chill. Lara's eyes were still so flooded with tears and it had become so very dark that she almost missed seeing the big tree. It suddenly loomed before them, so large that at first they thought it was a wall. Deep crevices were in its bark and they could barely make out overhead the enormous branches which were themselves as large as many of the surrounding trees. There was no time for considering alternatives, which was just as well. Had there been such time, Lara might well have been just as paralyzed with fear as she had been with the spell. She suddenly ducked down and, with muscles stiff, quietly moved in a crouch to the back of the cart and over the low tailgate.

Lara fell with a muted thump to the mossy, leaf-covered ground and was momentarily breathless but otherwise unhurt. She scrambled on all fours around the tree until out of sight of the cart and then crouched fearfully in the deep shade of a huge root. The muted rumbling of the cart quickly grew fainter and within a minute or so the sound was gone and she was all alone.

"I didn't even tell them goodbye," she thought and once again tears threatened to spill but she fought them back. She slowly stood up, listening. When no sound reached her ears, she began easing around the tree, which was even larger than she had thought. She moved along with her left hand against the craggy bark, the other hand brushing away limp streamers of moss hanging down from the branches. Every few feet she had to step over a large root. She had taken twenty full paces and was not quite halfway around the tree when one of the roots she was stepping over suddenly moved.

It was a very large black and red snake.

9

A Fight
in the Woods

LARA JUMPED BACK, gasping. Now, she was not really afraid of snakes and had even touched them in school, but those had been very small snakes, gentle and nonpoisonous. This one had a body bigger around than her own and she had no idea whether or not it was poisonous. And even if not poisonous, it could be a constrictor who could squeeze the breath out of her. Therefore, her reaction was entirely understandable.

The pattern of the snake's skin was like a checkerboard. One of his eyes, in the middle of a red square, was black; the other, in the middle of a black square, was red. At the end of his snout was a large ivory horn projecting straight up about two feet. The snake smoothly raised himself until he was higher than her own head, but it seemed certain that a great deal of his body was still hidden from sight in a large hole at the base of the giant tree. Part of the hole was in the tree and part in the ground.

"Sssso, here you are," the snake said softly. "You musssst be the one named Lara. Crobbity."

The little girl nodded until she could find her voice.

"Yes, I am. I don't mean to be rude, but you gave me a terrible scare."

"I'm sssso ssssorry," hissed the snake. "It'ssss hard not to sssscare people when everyone I encounter automatically expectssss the very worsssst. It issssn't really fair, but I've learned to live with it. You have nothing to fear. I am Trooom."

The snake's mouth, as he opened it to speak, was very wide and his deeply forked tongue was black on one side, red on the other. He did not have huge fangs as a poisonous snake does, but upper and lower jaws were lined with an array of jagged teeth, much like those of a shark.

Even as Trooom spoke, his body was sliding smoothly out of the large hole at the base of the tree. His eret head and foreparts remained where they were, but great loops of the body formed beyond them, disappearing in the darkness of the forest. Lara noticed that he was not wearing one of the torques.

"Crobbity, Mr. Trooom. If I may ask, how is it that you know my name?"

"Jusssst Trooom will do. You have an important friend who came to warn ussss of your predicament."

"Boggle?" Lara guessed, not knowing who else it might possibly be.

"Yessss," Trooom replied, nodding. "He came directly to Mag Namodder. I am to take you to her at onccccce."

"Mag Namodder? I believe Mr. Beadle mentioned her. Just who is she, Trooom?"

Trooom stared at her, as the final few yards of his great body slid from the hole. "You don't know? Why, sssshe issss the Foresssst Witch."

"A *witch?*" Lara's voice squeaked and her eyes grew very round.

"Well," said Trooom, "not just the Foressst Witch. Sssshe issss alsssso the Witch of the Hillssss and the Underland Witch and much more. Sssshe issss everything and her power issss almosssst unlimited."

Lara became very interested at this. "Really? Oh, Trooom, could she help me rescue Barnaby and William? They're my brother and cousin. The Centaurs are taking them to the castle and I'm afraid they might be killed."

"I have no doubt sssshe could, Lara. Assss to whether or not sssshe *would*, that issss ssssomething you will have to take up with her. Now, we'd better get go —"

"My Lady!"

The deep voice interrupted Trooom and just as abruptly there was a thump and a sharp twanging sound. An arrow was suddenly sticking deep in Trooom's exposed throat. Another thump and another. Two more arrows had struck, one high in Trooom's side and another close to the back of his head. Instantly he began writhing terribly but in spite of this he hissed a command to Lara.

"Go!" he gasped. "Into the hole. Quickly . . . on your life!"

Lara, still not having seen the enemy, leaped toward the big hole and plunged into it, her movement witnessed only by a yellow bird that had just glided in unseen and settled on a branch of the huge tree well off the ground. He nodded as he saw Lara dash into the hole and then turned his attention to what was happening to the snake.

Inside the hole, Lara found a very thick door so cleverly counterbalanced that she had no difficulty swinging it shut. It was disguised with bark on the outer surface so that, when shut, it was almost invisible in the forest dimness. Heavy latches automatically fell into place as soon as it was closed. At the same time a long narrow slit became visible in the door, through which Lara could see outside.

More arrows were striking Trooom and in the shadows beyond his writhing body were two of the Centaur guards, nocking the last of the arrows from their quivers onto their bowstrings. A third Centaur swept into view holding his broadsword aloft. His quiver was already empty and his bow slung over a shoulder. It was Tark.

As he reached the others, they let fly their final shafts. Both arrows hit their mark, as had the others. Hanging their bows over their shoulders, the pair drew their swords and fell in behind their leader as he galloped past, heading directly for Trooom.

"In the name of Thorkin!" they cried in unison.

The writhing of the huge snake had so diminished by now that he was almost motionless. He still held his head high off the ground, but was swaying and seemed on the point of collapsing. More than twenty arrows stuck out of his head and body and his tongue lolled from his mouth. The Centaurs were obviously rushing in for the kill, but they had gravely misjudged their adversary.

As Tark galloped up brandishing his sword, Trooom's head shot forward with blinding speed and his great jaws closed over the midpoint of Tark's body. The Centaur was lifted high off the ground, his hooves kicking furiously as a great shriek erupted from him. At the same moment the long thick body of Trooom lashed about, crashing against tree trunks and breaking off lower limbs. Huge loops of the snake's body collided with both of the other Centaurs and instantly Trooom threw several great coils around them and began squeezing with terrible pressure. The Centaurs screamed as their bodies were crushed.

Gripped in Trooom's mouth, Tark made one final thrust with his sword. The blade buried itself deeply in the snake's neck and Trooom fell over and died. Tark, too, was dead, his body still held tightly in Trooom's jaws.

Behind the heavy door, Lara began to sob and the tears filling her eyes prevented her from seeing the yellow bird leap into flight and speed away toward the mountains. She simply moaned aloud and turned away from the awful scene outside and sat down, burying her face in her hands. She was trembling badly and for a long while her sobbing echoed softly in the semidarkness.

After a while, Lara got control of herself and raised her head. She could not bear to look out through the slit or open the door again and so she turned her attention to the interior of the hole. There was more than enough room for her to stand and the earthen floor beneath her feet sloped gently downward before her. A pale greenish light emanated from the walls and when she looked more closely, she found that lichens were growing there and the source of the glow was from them.

With no other reasonable option apparent, she began following the passage. Soon the hole widened into a cave and earth gave way to solid rock. Even though she wore rubber-soled tennis shoes, every now and again she would scuff her foot or kick a small stone and the sound would echo hollowly. The cave was now wide enough to drive a large truck through. She felt very small and very alone. In view of what had happened between Trooom and the Centaurs, her fear for Barnaby and William had grown considerably. All that was important to her now was to find some way of saving them.

Soon the cave was angling downward at a much steeper pitch and walking would have been extremely difficult for Lara, except that now there was a broad flight of steps carved out of the rock. They were damp with water dripping from the cave's ceiling and she had to walk very carefully to keep from slipping. Far ahead she could see what appeared to be a broad landing and, dimly beyond that, a narrower arched passageway through solid rock. To one side of the archway was what appeared to be a peculiar rock formation on which had been painted diamond shapes of white and deep red. She took little note of it as she approached, however, her attention riveted to the arched passageway, the far end of which was brightly lighted. She was afraid someone or some *thing* was lurking in that dark tunnel and would spring out at her as she passed.

The stairs ended and she walked across the broad flat landing to the passage entry. There she stood, craning her neck and peering intently into the darkness that ended in brightness.

"Where issss Trooom?"

The deep voice so startled Lara that she gasped aloud and spun around. Behind her, suddenly between her and the stairs, was what she had mistaken for an oddly painted rock formation — another great snake. Except for the difference in color and pattern, he appeared to be identical to Trooom, even to the large ivory horn on his snout.

"Cr . . . cr . . . crobbity," Lara said, her heart pounding heavily.

"Where issss Trooom?" the snake repeated, his hissing voice resounding in the chamber with the sound of rushing water.

"I'm . . . I'm afraid he's . . ." Lara couldn't finish the sentence. "He was going to take me to Mag Namodder, but then the Centaurs came back. They shot him with arrows and he killed them but he . . . he . . ."

"He, too, wassss sssslain?"

"Yes sir. I'm so sorry."

"And you are the one called Lara?"

"Yes sir."

There was a long period when the snake did not speak, though a peculiar keening sound, half a cry, half a long wheezing sound, issued from him. Then he spoke softly, sadly, his voice a gentle sibilance in the dimness.

"He wassss my brother," said the snake, talking more to himself than to the girl. "He knew there could be danger, but it did not sssstop him. It wassss hissss way. Perhapsssss one day there will be a sssstatue erected to hissss memory. Heroesssss sssshould have sssstatuesssss.

Mag Namodder will grieve assss much assss I. I musssst go to her at oncccce."

Lara felt a surge of excitement. "Will you take me with you?" she asked.

"Of coursssse! And forgive me for not introduccccing mysssself. I am Krooom. Crobbity. Now, Lara," — he lowered his head until his chin was upon the landing — "pleasssse, climb onto my head. Ssssit with your legssss over my ssssnout and hold very tightly to my horn."

She did as bade, though with some difficulty, hooking her legs over Krooom's snout and wrapping her arms tightly around his horn. As soon as she was settled, Krooom moved forward smoothly into the passage. It became brighter and brighter the closer they approached the far end. Then they were there and Krooom stopped on a great platform of rock jutting from the sheer wall of an incredibly immense cavern. Looking upward, Lara could not see the ceiling, since a dense layer of brilliant mist or clouds hid it. The bright light, of the same intensity as far as she could see, seemed to emanate from the clouds themselves. That, however, was not what made her suck in her breath in surprise.

They were so high she was immediately dizzy and she tightened her grip around Krooom's horn even more. Far, far below — perhaps a mile or better below them — were beautiful green fields and a multitude of tiny lakes of brilliant shimmering blue. And in the midst of this

"Well now," said the little man, setting a tray on the low table before them, *"let's refresh ourselves and get acquainted"* (page 53).

The snake smoothly raised himself until he was higher than her own head, but it seemed certain that a great deal of his body was still hidden from sight in a large hole at the base of the giant tree (page 80).

lovely scene was a city of considerable size, dominated by a huge castle. Its walls and towers were pure white and its many roofs on different levels were sparkling green.

"Welcome, Lara," Krooom hissed softly, "to Twilandia."

10

The Regal Dart

BARNABY AND WILLIAM, meanwhile, were not faring any too well. They had been very frightened when Lara scrambled off the back of the cart in the darkest part of the woods.

"Well, it looks like she made it all right," William had whispered, after several minutes had passed and the little procession had not faltered.

"The least she could have done," grumbled Barnaby, also whispering, "was say goodbye."

That might have sounded a little selfish, but he didn't mean it that way. He was very worried that she would fall into greater danger, with no one to help her, and that he would never see her again.

"There wasn't time," William murmured. "But she'll be all right. She's got a lot more guts than I gave her credit for at first. And I know she'll do all she possibly can to help us."

William wasn't as confident as he sounded. Inside, he was just as worried about her as Barnaby and, actually, he had very little faith that they would ever be reunited. This feeling became much stronger when, after another few minutes, Tark suddenly detached himself from the other Centaurs and came thudding back toward the cart.

There was still so little daylight here that it wasn't until the leader of the Centaurs was directly beside the cart that he discovered Lara was missing. At first he evidently thought she had toppled over and was lying on the floor of the vehicle, so he craned his head to look down into it. When she was nowhere to be seen, his anger burst out full bloom.

"Halt!" he ordered loudly. "The girl is gone!" He turned his attention to the boys as the cart stopped and the five other Centaurs came back to cluster around their leader and peek over the board sides.

"Tark's right," said one.

"He sure is," said another.

"The girl's really gone," said a third.

"Disappeared," said the fourth.

"What'll we do now, Tark?" asked the fifth.

"We'll *find* her, that's what," said their leader. "You there!" He pointed at William. "How did she get away?"

William didn't answer.

"Who lifted the spell?"

William didn't answer.

"How long has she been gone?"

Still William said nothing.

Angrily, Tark put his hand on William's head and shoved him and the boy toppled over into the bottom of the cart, still in his running position. Other than a soft grunt when he hit, William made no sound.

Tark turned his attention to Barnaby. "Where did she go?"

Barnaby said nothing.

"Who helped her?"

Barnaby said nothing.

"Answer me!"

Still Barnaby remained silent, and Tark shoved him just as angrily. Barnaby also toppled over and landed on top of William, causing both boys to grunt, and then his momentum made him roll off his cousin and they both lay in their paralyzed positions in the bottom of the cart.

"King Thorkin will have our heads for this!" Tark said to his fellows. "We have to find her. You and you," he pointed, "come with me. You other three, move on with the prisoners. Blix," he added, pointing at the largest of the three, "you'll be in charge of the detachment. Your job is to get them to the castle. One of you ride behind and keep an eye on these two. Just keep going. We'll overtake you later with the girl . . . or with her head, if need be!"

He moved with his two companions in the direction from which they had come, staring at the ground for any sign of where Lara got off. The three moved like shadows, without any whisper of sound coming from beneath their hooves.

Now Barnaby and William were truly terrified. Lara had climbed off the cart such a short time ago that they were sure the Centaurs would quickly catch her, or maybe even kill her. Barnaby began to cry and William tried to comfort him at first, but soon he was crying, too.

In a moment Blix gave a command and the boys felt the cart begin moving again, but from this point on they saw very little of their surroundings. They could see the trees overhead while they were in the woods, the daylight becoming deep lavender-green as it filtered through the leaves. Also, they could see the pale green sky when they left the woods and descended the treeless hills, but that was all. They didn't talk much, both of them dreading the sound of the returning hoofbeats of Tark and his two followers. But the journey went on for several hours and the absent Centaurs did not show up. Even the three Centaurs escorting the cart became worried and the boys could hear Blix talking with his companions, wondering what was keeping Tark and the others.

They went through several more groves of trees, mainly going gradually downhill and then, at length, into a very extensive forest. After another hour of bumping through the forest they came into bright daylight again. The rumble of the wooden wheels became very loud and then stopped.

"I think we've moved onto a platform of some kind, Barnaby," William whispered.

Barnaby nodded, but not until Blix gave an order and the boys were lifted out of the cart by the other two Centaurs, were they able to determine their situation.

They saw now that they were on a wharf jutting from shore into the waters of Green Lake. A dozen or more stone pedestals, each holding on its top the skull of a person or strange creature, were located at intervals on the wharf and along the shoreline. A few of those along the shore were leaning and several had toppled over and lay as they fell, unheeded. All of these statues were very stained from exposure.

The attention of the boys was more taken, however, by the large single-masted ship that was moored to the wharf. It was very wide, with banks of oars on each side and, on the prow, a huge wooden figurehead of a bearded man wearing a crown and pointing a great sword forward. Its furled sail, lashed to the boom, was purple and the ship itself was white with purple trim. On its bow were painted the words REGAL DART.

"Wow," said Barnaby, as he and William were stood upright on the wharf, "look at that!"

"Looks as if they're going to take us aboard that ship," William said.

He was correct, of course. During the next few minutes the empty cart, escorted by one of the Centaurs, was pulled by the stag off the wharf and disappeared into the woods bordering the lake. In turn, Barnaby and William were picked up and carried across the board gangplank and onto an elevated deck at the stern, the hooves of the Centaurs galump-galumping over the wood.

They were met there by the captain, a burly Gnome with powerful arms and short sturdy legs. His nose was remarkably long and his ears came to points at both top and bottom. A dense growth of curly black beard covered cheeks and jaws and framed his wide mouth. His eyes were small and very dark and his thick eyebrows formed a continuous line from the left side of his face to the right. His clothing was all black, from his cap with a floppy top covering the back of his head to shoes whose tips curved upward and back toward his ankles. The clothing he wore was one-piece, open at the neck, exposing curly black hair on his chest and a torque around his throat. The garment was long-sleeved, snug at wrists and just below his knees, but his lower legs were bare. A huge curved knife was in a belt sheath and in his right hand he held a coiled whip.

"Ah *hah!*" he chortled as the Centaurs completed placing the boys on the deck. "Prisoners, eh? Do you want them lashed? Do you want them put in irons? We can keel-haul 'em, once we're under way. Or hang 'em by their thumbs from the yardarm. Ever tell you about the time we hung three Dwirgs and a Satyr who —"

"Never mind that, Captain Greeb," replied the spokesman of the three Centaurs. "These are King

Thorkin's prisoners and nothing is to happen to them except by royal order."

"Oh fudge!" said the Gnome, swatting his own leg with the coiled whip and eyeing the two boys. "Always someone to spoil the fun. I suppose that means we're heading for the castle now? Reminds me of the time we made the renegade Centaur walk the plank. Now that was somethi—"

"Yes," the Centaur broke in, "to the castle." He had been wondering if he should wait for the return of Tark, but now decided against it. Something had happened, he was sure of it. Otherwise they would have caught up long ago. "Yes," he repeated. "At once. I'm afraid Tark is lost."

Captain Greeb's long eyebrow went up. "Is that a fact?" A gravelly laughter rumbled from his barrel chest. "Too bad. How'd it happen? Beheaded? Impaled? Crushed? Wish I'd been there to see it. Always miss the good stuff. Ever tell you abou—"

"Just get this ship underway, Captain, *now!*"

"What a sorehead!" the Gnome muttered, but he immediately turned and began to issue orders to his crew. The gangplank was raised and ropes mooring the ship to the wharf were slipped. A harsh order was shouted, relayed by crew members and accompanied by the cracking of the whips. The rowers dipped their long oars at once and the ship began moving out into the lake.

It was the first time Barnaby and William had really

noticed the other prisoners. There were about sixty of them, two by two, on short benches on each side of the ship. They were chained ankle to ankle and were the strangest group of people the boys had ever seen. There were Dwarfs and Gnomes, Satyrs and Fauns, Elves and Dryads, Nyads, Imps and others the boys could not recognize. Members of the crew, all of them Gnomes, were striding back and forth among the rowers, occasionally using their whips to lash the backs of those they thought were not working hard enough. Or perhaps just for the sport of it.

"I think we're in trouble," Barnaby said to his cousin.

"We've *been* in trouble ever since we entered that stupid turnstile," William replied. "We're just getting into it deeper all the time."

"There's one thing we can be thankful for," Barnaby said.

"What?"

"Tark and the others didn't come back. They think he's lost. Maybe that means Lara got away."

"I hope so!" William said fervently.

As the *Regal Dart* moved out of the more protected waters, a breeze began rippling the surface of the lake. Once again the boys noticed that there was no reflection on the water, though the sun was shining brightly. With the ripples quickly turning into small waves, Captain Greeb shouted an order for the rowers to reef their oars and the sail to be hoisted.

Several of the Gnomes began climbing the rigging and one took a position in the crow's nest. A half dozen or so other Gnomes unlashed the sail and tugged at a thick rope. Foot by foot the sail was raised to its limit. It caught the wind and bellied out and now William and Barnaby could see that it was not only purple, there was an emblem on it: a huge head of a full-bearded man in the center of a white circle.

The ship picked up speed and skimmed swiftly across the surface. It angled out to the middle of Green Lake and then the helmsman, obeying an order barked by Captain Greeb, shoved against the tiller and the ship took a new course down the length of the huge lake, heading toward the far-distant Gray Mountains.

For half an hour there was only the sound of the ship creaking and the rigging slapping against the mast and

the sail popping. Then, from far above, a cry came from the lookout.

"Castle Thorkin off starboard bow!"

A cheer went up from the crew and the helmsman took a direct line bearing for the huge structure on the distant shore ahead. Within another ten minutes they were close enough to see the castle quite well. It loomed like a great cliff at the water's edge, its turrets towering high above the trees of the forest beyond it. The barren Gray Mountains rose just beyond the trees. Small purple flags with white circles in the center flapped atop poles on each of the castle's towers and William was sure that on closer inspection each of the white circles would have a bearded man's head in the center. The thick walls were of gloomy gray-black stone and there were few windows.

Hundreds of sailboats with furled sails were anchored in the protective harbor before the castle, most of them smaller than the *Regal Dart*. As their own ship came closer, Barnaby and William realized that the castle was not on the mainland but rather it occupied almost the entire surface of a sizeable island several hundred yards from the nearest shore. A causeway projected out from the mainland shore toward the castle and a large drawbridge, lowerable from the castle wall, connected the causeway to the island.

"Pilot approaching!" cried the lookout.

Everyone looked where he was pointing. A bird had just launched itself from one of the turrets and was speeding toward them. In less than two minutes it reached them, circled the ship once and then alighted on the boom close to where the skipper was standing. It was a bird not much larger than a small chicken, with bright yellow plumage.

"That's the same kind of bird as Boggle," William murmured.

"He sure looks just like Boggle," Barnaby murmured back.

The bird fluffed its feathers, preened self-consciously for a moment and then stood straight and saluted Captain Greeb. "Pilot on board, Cap'n. Ready to take 'er in."

"Then do it and be quick," grumbled Captain Greeb, "or we'll have spitted and barbecued yellow bird for dinner tonight."

"Aye aye, sir!" The bird filled his lungs with a great inhalation and then uttered a piercing, three-noted whistle similar to one that William once heard in a movie about the Navy. "Now hear this!" the bird shrieked. "Bring 'er about! Lower your mains'l! Clear your fo'c'sle! Trim your jib. Pipe your deck call! Batten your hatches! Ready your oars! Shiver your timbers! Open your —"

"Belay there!" roared Captain Greeb. "Just pilot us in to our mooring."

"He sure acts just like Boggle," Barnaby said.

"Those yellow birds must all act that way," William muttered back.

"Aye aye, sir!" said the bird crisply. "I'll pilot you in like no one's ever piloted you in before. I'll pilot you past the reefs. I'll pilot you around the shoals. I'll pilot you over the oyster beds. You've never seen such a job of piloting as you'll get today. Why, I'll pilot —"

"DO IT!" the captain bellowed.

"He sure sounds just like Boggle," Barnaby said.

"I guess they all *sound* alike too," William muttered back.

"Aye aye, sir!" the yellow bird said and began piloting the ship into the crowded harbor. But before he did so, and while the captain was engaged in a low conversation with the Centaur, the bird cocked his head and looked toward the two boys. He bowed low toward them and then sent them a broad wink.

"He *is* Boggle!" the boys whispered in unison.

11

Castle Thorkin

AS SOON AS the *Regal Dart* was skillfully brought to its mooring at the Castle Thorkin wharf, William and Barnaby were carried ashore by the two Centaurs and brought into the castle courtyard through the watergate. There were dozens and dozens of skulls of people and creatures mounted atop stone pedestals. Many had obviously been there a long time and were stained by mildew or weather, while others looked relatively new. The skulls were largely ignored by the scores of living people and creatures of various types who were milling about.

All the people were wearing torques; and as the group from the *Regal Dart* passed them, they stopped their milling about and gathered in a loose crowd to watch. None of these people said a word and they parted respectfully to let the Centaurs through, William carried by Blix, Barnaby by the other. Boggle was riding on the back of Blix and remained there as the two boys were carefully lowered to the broad stone patio before the main entrance to the gigantic castle.

The cousins were so stunned by what they were seeing that they were speechless, which was just as well, since Boggle had whispered urgently to them just before they were taken off the ship.

"Say nothing unless spoken to," he had murmured, "and do not offer any information. You should be safe for a while, provided Lady Lara is not caught."

As soon as they deposited the boys on the patio, the three Centaurs took an alert, expectant stance close to them, one on each side and one behind. The murmuring of the crowd stilled and everyone seemed to be waiting for something to happen. Most were looking at the great portal of the castle.

Two life-sized statues of upright snarling bears flanked the entry. The huge arched doors were twenty feet high and elaborately carved with representations of stags and unicorns and boars, plus a great deal of scrollwork. Two guards were at the doorway, each holding a spear, point up, with the butt end resting on the ground. At the sound of a chorus of trumpets, they turned and pulled open the massive doors just enough to allow two men to walk out, followed in single file by half a dozen servants.

One of the men was elderly and he walked slowly with the aid of a crooked staff. His long white beard was draped over one shoulder and trailed halfway down his back. Great bushy gray eyebrows formed miniature storm clouds over deepset eyes and his nose was small and sharply pointed. He wore a dark maroon robe that just barely touched the ground, belted at his waist with a gold rope with tasseled ends. The cowl of his robe came to a small peak, but he tossed it back off his head as they approached the paralyzed boys. William and Barnaby could now see that he had a smooth bald dome with a fringe of gray hair half around his head in back and his large ears were very prominent.

The other individual was quite a handsome young man not more than seven or eight years older than William. His hair was dark and he moved with the grace of an athlete. He was elegantly dressed in an immaculate white silk blouse and dark blue tights. Fine spun gold slippers covered his feet and a sheathed dagger with exquisitely carved hasp was held by his wide belt of woven gold. Both he and the old man wore torques.

The two came to a stop several feet in front of the boys and looked them over closely, staring in particular at their bare necks. Then the old man scowled and looked up from beneath his shaggy eyebrows at the Centaurs.

"Which one of you is in charge?" he asked.

"Crobbity, Magnificence. I was placed in charge by Tark," said their leader, stepping forward with some degree of nervousness. Boggle, still perched on his back, seemed on the point of falling asleep.

"And who are you?"

"My name is Blix."

"Where is Tark? More importantly, where is the girl?"

Blix became more uncomfortable and shifted his feet. "As we passed through the Deep Woods he went back to check on her and found her gone."

"Escaped!" The old man was furious. "How? Wasn't she under the Spell of *Ossyfia*?"

"She was," admitted Blix, "so perhaps she was carried off, rather than escaped. Whatever the case, she was gone. Tark went with two others to overtake her and bring her back. He told me to continue and he would catch up. He didn't, Magnificence. I fear the worst."

Though they tried not to do so, William and Barnaby smiled, relief once again washing through them that Lara had not been caught. The old man's eyes flicked toward them and his anger increased. He reached out with his staff and tapped each of them once atop the head. The blows were hard enough to raise a lump and cause tears to fill their eyes.

"Consider yourselves fortunate," he rasped. "Those who irk me usually fare much worse. Do you know who I am?"

"Mr. Magnificence?" ventured Barnaby hesitantly, wishing he could rub the bump on his head.

The old man looked at him sharply, eyes smoldering, searching for any trace of insolence. Discovering none, he relaxed a little, though he still appeared very threatening.

"I am Warp," he said. "Chief of WAAS."

"We don't know what that means, sir," William said.

"Not only impertinent but stupid, too, eh?" Warp drew himself up straighter. "WAAS is the Mesmerian Department of Wizardry, Astrology and Sorcery. I have spells I have not yet even used, so don't tempt me to use them on you!"

The younger man was showing signs of impatience. "There is only one spell called for at this time, Warp," he said, the ring of authority in his voice. "I suggest you invoke the Spell of *Metasta* on them immediately so we may approach the throne. It would be most unwise to keep His Majesty waiting."

The wizard stared at him a moment and then dipped his head with poor grace. "Of course, Prince Daw," he said.

He pointed his staff at the boys and murmured a brief incantation in a language the boys could not understand. Instantly a pale blue aura surrounded the two youngsters. It lasted for no more than three seconds and when it faded away, their paralysis was gone, along with all the aches and pains and stiffness they had been experiencing from being so long in one position. Even the lump that had been raised on the head of each with the staff was gone, along with the pain. They were greatly relieved.

"Follow us," Prince Daw commanded Blix.

The young man turned and, with Warp beside him, walked toward the door. The servants fell in behind them. Blix issued brief commands and followed, William and Barnaby behind him, delighted to be able to move under their own power again, and the other Centaur brought up the rear. As soon as they entered, the doors were shut behind them with a deep echoing boom, causing Boggle to stir sleepily on the Centaur's back and lift his head briefly.

"Whuzzit? Whuzzit?" he murmured. "Who's making all the noise? What's going on? Who's doing what? Who closed the doors? Where are we going? What's happening? Somebody got a message for me to carry?"

"Boggle, be quiet!" Blix said gruffly, looking back over his shoulder in an annoyed way. "And find someplace else to ride."

"Yessir, yessir!" Boggle said, straightening. "I'll do that. I'll find someplace else to ride right away. Quite the thing to do. Quite."

He stretched out his wings and lofted himself smoothly into the air, circled twice and then came to rest on William's right shoulder and close to Barnaby, who was walking directly beside his cousin on the right. At once he settled down in his sleepy manner again, his eyes half closed.

The hooves of the Centaurs resounded through the great stone chambers through which the party was walking. A few people, mainly servants, were moving about and paused to watch as the little party went by. They passed through several archways, each leading to a different chamber. Stairways, some angled and some spiral, went up or down here and there, evidently leading to rooms out of sight to the group. Massive hewn stone pillars were passed at intervals and there were hideous skulls of people and animals. At last they stopped before a wide double door made of iron, at which Warp pointed his staff.

"*Dehisce!*" he commanded.

At once the doors swung wide to an enormous room about as large as a football field, with a very high ceiling. The windows were only tall narrow slits high up the walls and open to the outside. A great din of voices met them. In addition to ordinary people, primarily in peasant dress, there were at least a hundred Gnomes and Elves and Dwarfs of several types, along with a scattering of Centaurs, Fauns and Satyrs. Among the most numerous of all were members of a race of tall thin people with light blue skin, long red hair and pleasant features. There were also a number of stocky furry animals which looked like wolverines, and about as many shaggy bears, their dense coats speckled white on black.

A half-dozen or more large, gray, fiercely toothed lizards with huge eyes covered by enormous sunglasses were standing upright on their hind legs, the front legs small and apparently used more like arms than legs. Heavy overlapping scales covered their bodies like armor and their long narrow tails were coiled like bullwhips behind them. Twenty or so large birds with dark greenish-black plumage stood in a cluster by themselves, looking like a group of robed monks. Their beaks were very large and savagely hooked, their curved talons tapering to needle points, the forward edge of their wings comprised of a horny sawtoothed material. They, too, had great saucer-like eyes, which appeared to be completely dark amber in color, without pupils. Everyone in the room, whether human or animal, so far as the boys could determine, was wearing a torque.

As the thick iron doors thudded shut behind the new arrivals, they immediately became the center of attention. The din of conversation became somewhat subdued, though continuing with a more excited undercurrent now at seeing two boys who were not wearing torques. The crowd parted to let them pass slowly toward the head of the room where there was a dais, upon which there was a large ornate throne with a smaller throne on each side. Several times the word "death" could be heard and a resurgence of fear sprang up in the boys.

Boggle was still perched sleepily on William's shoul-

der, his head couched deeply in his plumage. His eyes were only half open, but there was more alertness in them than anyone realized. He sensed the boys' fear rising anew and, without moving except to open his beak slightly, he spoke in a whisper that reached only the two cousins.

"Chin up, now," he said, with forced cheerfulness. "Chin up. Just take things as they come. You'll be all right."

"Who are all these people?" William whispered back.

"They are primarily representatives of the subjects of King Thorkin," Boggle replied. "They have come here representing their individual provinces to pay homage to their King. At least that's what Thorkin calls it. Actually, it is tax time and they've come from all over Mesmeria to pay their taxes."

"How much do they have to pay?" Barnaby asked softly, smart enough to keep facing forward and hardly moving his lips.

"The usual government rate," Boggle replied matter-of-factly. "Three times more than anyone can afford."

They were only partially through the crowd when their forward progress was stopped as Prince Daw and Warp paused to speak to the leader of the fierce-looking lizards.

Barnaby gasped faintly as he got a better look at the scaly creatures. "What are *those?*" he hissed.

"Crepuscular Krins," Boggle murmured. "Very dangerous people. Like the nocturnal Vulpines over there," he tilted his head slightly toward the cluster of big-eyed birds, "who're also dangerous, they're Dymzonians. Actually, they're exempt from taxes, since they're not Mesmerians, but they're here in the service of King Thorkin."

"Doing what?" Barnaby persisted.

"Bodyguards for one thing. Spies for another. Very treacherous people." Boggle sniffed distastefully. "They spy on their own people and each other's in Dymzonia and report to Thorkin. Sometimes they even make forays into Darkland to do some spying there. A state of war has existed between Mesmeria and Darkland for as long as anyone can remember. And Dymzonians are at war with both; that's why they're so fierce."

"But why are the crepuscular Krins," William asked,

stumbling slightly over the words, "wearing sunglasses?"

"Their home territory exists in a state of perpetual twilight," Boggle explained. "Even though they occupy the lightest quadrant of Dymzonia, it is still only the light of deep twilight. They can see perfectly in those areas where light levels are very low, and even reasonably well in Darkland, but their eyes are too sensitive to tolerate direct daylight."

"Well, then, what about the nocturnal Vulpines?"

"They occupy the darkest quadrant of Dymzonia — not true darkness as in Darkland, but close to it. They can see quite satisfactorily in Darkland. Considerably better than the Krins."

"If that's the case," Barnaby spoke up, "then how come the Vulpines aren't wearing sunglasses like those the Krins have to wear?"

"Because they're physically better adapted. They have nictitating membranes."

"Nicti . . . what?"

"Nictitating membranes. They're like extra eyelids that slide up over the eyes and protect them. They're dark in color but transparent, so they become, in essence, built-in sunglasses. They —"

He was abruptly interrupted by heavy booming sounds. An instantaneous hush settled over the room as a guard standing on a wooden platform at the right front of the room thumped the butt of his heavy spear on the hollow flooring three times. He followed this with an announcement in a deep strong voice.

"His Royal Majesty, the King! Ruler of Mesmeria and all its protectorates. Tamer of the Tempest Ocean! Conqueror of the World! Lord of all living creatures!"

William and Barnaby stared at one another and Barnaby's lower lip began to tremble. The moment was at hand when they would be face to face with the dreaded King Thorkin.

12

King Thorkin's Taxes

A HIDDEN DOORWAY opened in the front corner of the great hall of Castle Thorkin and four guards entered, two by two. Each was dressed in chain mail and each bore an unsheathed sword with a wide black blade. Immediately behind them emerged King Thorkin, followed by four more of the guards similarly clad and armed. At once, everyone in the room bowed very low and remained that way. Everyone, that is, except William and Barnaby. Boggle, still on William's shoulder, was bowing and now he whispered to them urgently.

"Bow! Hurry! If you value your lives, *bow*. Do it!"

They did as the yellow bird bade them, though only far enough that they could still glimpse the monarch from under their brows.

Without looking left or right, King Thorkin strode with deliberate paces to the dias, each step of his approach becoming more menacing in the silence that prevailed. They were not loud steps, only very sinister in the stillness. At the principal throne he stopped, facing his audience. He was a large man with a full beard and the boys realized that the figurehead on the boat and the emblem on its sail and on the castle flags were representations of this man. He was clad in elephant-gray trousers and shirt and a half-cape of soft gray fur lined with crimson silk. Black suede knee boots covered his lower legs and he wore a breastplate of beaten iron. A crown of dull gold set with unpolished gemstones rested on his head. In one big hand he clenched a short scepter fashioned not of gold but rather of dull gray iron — an inch-thick rod with a fist-sized ball at the end.

As soon as Thorkin seated himself on the throne, the guard on the wooden platform thumped his spear shaft a single time. As the dull booming resounded through the great chamber, everyone straightened, but silence still prevailed. The monarch let his gaze sweep across the assemblage, pausing briefly at Warp and Prince Daw and the Centaurs and two prisoners behind them, then moving on.

"My minister of finance and taxation," he said loudly, "has inspected the coffers newly replenished with the tribute you have brought from your various peoples and in most cases, the obligations have been fully met. But," he added, his brow becoming a deep frown, "there are several who have fallen short in this respect. The principal representatives of the following districts will now approach the throne: the Voley District of Mellafar, the Knogg District of Verdancia, the Dwaerg District of Selerdor and both the Tworpestia and Rufolia Districts of Rubiglen."

There was a stirring in the crowd as five individuals made their way to the front of the room. They aligned themselves before the throne, where they stood silently. Warp and Prince Daw also had gone forward, but respectfully bowed to Thorkin and then seated themselves on the smaller thrones to left and right of the monarch's. For a moment the king studied the five individuals standing twenty feet in front of him. Then he sighed and nodded to Warp.

"In the great benevolence of his nature," Warp said, his powerful voice carrying well throughout the vast room, "and with sympathetic ear, His Majesty will now entertain brief explanations from these assembled representatives as to why their tax quotas were not met." He pointed to the individual to the far left in the line. "We will begin with Ferric, who is standing in for the absent representative of the Rufolia District of Rubiglen."

Ferric, a middle-aged man with weathered face and gnarled hands, took a step forward, bowed and addressed himself to the King, whose demeanor had become stern. "Your Excellency, severe storms ruined many of our crops only a few weeks ago, just at harvest time. Our absent representative of this district, Holta Weedie, is himself ill with a severe fever. Full payment of the taxes will be made just as soon as possible." He bowed again and stepped back into the line.

"Representative Mus of the Voley District of Mellafar," announced Warp.

A short, lean man with a very pointed, rat-like face and small dark eyes stepped forward and bowed as Ferric had done. He brushed nervously at his moustache and smiled weakly, exposing large buckteeth. "Your Majesty, against my wishes and advice, the citizens of my district have directed me to tell you — which I do most respectfully and only at their insistence — that they feel the taxes have become too much to bear. They say they will pay the same as they paid last year and no more." He backed away to his position in the line, bowing at every step.

"Representative Tunk of the Knogg District of Verdancia," said Warp.

Tunk was a Faun, no taller than Mus. From the waist down he was goatlike, with narrow lower legs and delicate hooves and a dense coat of curly dark gray hair. Above the waist he was human, except for the pair of short, upward curving horns which projected from his hairline at the sides of his forehead. His voice, when he spoke, was shrill and he seemed to be having difficulty keeping his temper under control.

"Your Excellency," he said, "you portray yourself as a benevolent king, but the taxation of your subjects is tyrannical. We cannot — we *will not* — pay!" His eyes were flashing and he seemed ready to say more, but then he merely dipped his head slightly and resumed his place in the line.

Warp's glance flicked to King Thorkin, whose features remained set in stern lines. "Representative Teedy of the Dwaerg District of Selerdor," Warp said.

Teedy was a Dwirg, one of the several races of Dwarfs inhabiting Mesmeria. Only three feet tall, he had a long, comically flexible nose and large green eyes that might have given him a mournful expression save for the laughter crinkles at their outer corners. His complexion was ruddy and his shoulder-length hair was strawberry blond. He wore short pants with broad suspenders and his bare feet were horny with calluses. He bowed so low that the tip of his nose touched the floor.

"My King," he said, his voice surprisingly low and rumbling for such a little person, "my constituents have asked me to explain to you that, though we would willingly do so if it were possible, there are no means by which we can meet the recently imposed increase in taxes. We have paid the same as we paid the last time, which was more than we could comfortably afford. We cannot pay what we do not have." He bowed deeply again and returned to the line.

"Finally," Warp said, "Representative Roo-Too of the Tworpestia District of Rubiglen."

Roo-Too was the only woman of the five. She was a Tworp, that race of thin, blue-skinned people with long red hair. Her features were delicate but there was a steely quality in her manner. Her deep blue eyes stared unflinchingly into the monarch's as she stepped up before the throne.

"King Thorkin," she began, "what none of the representatives before me has said, but which they all feel, is this: your taxes are unfair, unjust, punitive and reprehensible. You squeeze your subjects as if they were fruit from which you mean to extract every drop of juice. No more! The Tworps make up a large percentage of the Mesmerian army and serve you faithfully in that capacity, for which they receive almost nothing in return except the right to pay taxes." Her fiery gaze switched to Prince Daw, who was ruler of the entire province of Rubiglen, then back to Thorkin. "Tworpestia serves official notice at this moment. Henceforth, we will pay only one-half of the tax we have been paying heretofore!"

There was a shocked silence as Roo-Too turned without bowing and strode back to her place in the line. Prince Daw had become very pale and Warp had risen and was in the process of pointing his staff at her when Thorkin raised a hand, staying him. The King came to his feet and his gaze fastened on the replacement representative from Rufolia.

"Ferric," he said, "taxation cannot be based upon the whims of nature. Nevertheless, we sympathize with you in the loss of your crops and our lenience is hereby reflected in a penalty that is unusually moderate. Our judgment is this: You will be given an extension of one hundred days to pay the taxes due. If not paid at that time, five Rufolians will be executed. At the end of each week thereafter, if taxes are not paid, an additional five will be executed. By royal edict, I hereby proclaim you the new official representative of Rufolia. Representative Holta Weedie, for failing to appear before his King at the prescribed time, is hereby sentenced to life imprisonment in the Dismal Depths."

A collective gasp came from the crowd. The Dismal Depths were the awful dungeons located beneath Castle Thorkin. Unspeakable tortures were perpetrated on those unfortunates sentenced to go there. Prince Daw, features distorted with his consternation, leaped to his feet.

"Your Highness!" he said. "Your decision is most extreme, considering the situa—"

"Be seated!" thundered the King. "Hold your tongue or you will find yourself sharing the penalty."

Swallowing, Prince Daw backed down and slowly resumed his seat, gripping the ornate arms of the smaller throne until his knuckles turned white.

On William's shoulder, Boggle gave a little grunt and

And most surprised of all was Barnaby, because it was from his own throat that the word had burst forth (page 123).

*She felt great taloned toes snap down and encircle her like a basket
and she was lifted and carried away (page 178).*

shook his head sadly. The two boys were momentarily stunned. It was Barnaby who found his voice first.

"That's a moderate penalty?" he whispered.

"That's showing leniency?" William said.

The yellow bird nodded. "For King Thorkin, yes. But I think he's about to get tough."

Boggle was only too right. In turn, King Thorkin pointed at Mus, Tunk and Teedy, ordering them to step forward. Quaking, they obeyed, facing him in a trembling cluster. The King leaned over and whispered to Warp and the old wizard's lips curved up in a grim smile as he nodded. Thorkin straightened and looked at the three before him.

"For defying your King," he said coldly, "there is a fitting punishment."

The three trembled even more, drawing closer together, their eyes wide and their faces showing of abject fear. It was at this moment that Thorkin pointed the ball of his scepter at them and invoked a spell.

"*MONDU!*"

Instantly a jagged bolt of intense blue-white electricity shot from the ball, forked into three parts and struck them simultaneously with a horrendous crackling sound. Teedy, Tunk and Mus, faces distorted with terror and bodies clinging together in their fear, turned black, then cherry red. A wave of heat emanated from them and those onlookers who were closest shrank back, shielding their eyes. The red quickly faded to a dull gray and just as quickly the heat was gone. Bit by bit, hard chunks of blackened material that had been clothing and living flesh peeled away and fell to the floor, quickly diminishing to an ugly gray ash. Within two minutes, only the skeletons of the three remained standing, still clinging to one another. Then even the skeletons disintegrated into ash and the skulls plopped into the midst of the ashes and lay there open-mouthed and sightless, an awful reminder of what the three had so recently been.

Warp motioned to a group of three Centaurs standing to one side with the crowd. They trotted to him immediately, though obviously uneasy. The sorcerer murmured to them and the three turned and approached the skulls. Simultaneously they stooped and each picked up a skull. With their grisly burdens, the three moved together through the crowd toward the iron door. Their leader cried "*Dehisce!*" as they approached the portal. It opened smoothly and then closed again after they had passed through. A long shuddering sigh swept across the assemblage.

"Let that be a lesson," Warp cried, silencing them, "for any who would defy their King. They are now only skulls that will be placed permanently in the courtyard inside the main entrance as a reminder of what the penalty can be for anything less than instant and total obedience."

King Thorkin now turned his attention to Roo-Too. He raised his scepter and pointed the ball at her. "Yours," he grated, "will be an end even worse and far more painful!"

"*No!*"

The single word erupted from the crowd with such searing intensity and power that everyone froze. King Thorkin's eyes widened. Warp's jaw dropped and his mouth became a dark O. Prince Daw clasped his hands together in a prayerful attitude beneath his chin. Roo-Too spun around to look in an astonished way toward the source of the cry. Boggle was so surprised that for perhaps the only time in his life, he was speechless. William was even more stunned than that.

And most surprised of all was Barnaby, because it was from his own throat that the word had burst forth.

13

Mag Namodder

UNDOUBTEDLY you are wondering what has happened to Lara while all these things have been going on, so now we will find out. She had gasped when she saw Twilandia stretched out a mile or more below the ledge and hugged her arms around Krooom's horn even more tightly. She shivered with fright at being so high and the huge red-and-white snake felt this and did his best to reassure her.

"There issss nothing to fear, Lara," he told her gently. "Take three deep breathssss and let them out sssslowly and you will feel better."

She did as bade and felt remarkably better by the time she was finished.

"My goodness, Krooom," she said, still excited but no longer afraid, "however will we be able to get down there?"

"Quite ssssimple," he told her. "Hang on now. Here we go."

As he said this, Krooom wedged his tail tightly in the tunnel mouth and moved forward until two-thirds of his great body was stretched out at a downward angle over open space. Then his muscles tensed and from a point just a few feet in back of his head his body began to flatten. It became flatter and flatter and wider and wider until it was like a great broad ribbon in a diamond-shaped red-and-white pattern. Then he released his tail hold and the remainder of his body slid over the edge. As they began falling, he undulated his body in an up-and-down manner and immediately their fall turned into a long graceful glide just like a ribbon fluttering in the breeze. Their speed increased and Lara's ponytailed hair flowed backward from her head. It was not hard for her to hang on, however, since the upright horn she was clinging to broke the force of the wind.

"Ohhh, this is wonderful, Krooom," she said loudly over the rush of the air.

"Yessss, it issss," he hissed. "I've alwayssss loved to fly, ever ssssince I did my ssssolo flight as a youngsssster. Trooom and I often flew together, but I never did assss well assss he."

He fell silent then, lost in the memories shared with his brother, and Lara respected his feelings and said nothing more for a while. They glided in long sweeping curves, steeply at first but then leveling off as they came within a few hundred feet of the ground. The fields were neat squares of emerald green and gold separated from one another either by wooden fences with white-painted pickets or low walls of dark green stone. Trees with huge green leaves provided pleasant patches of shade and all the roads and paths that led toward the city were lined on each side with stately fir trees.

The city itself, as they made a pass above it, was a delight to see. The few walls and many buildings were constructed of cut pieces of stone, white as alabaster, and the shingles on the rooftops were a vivid green. Many people walking about below them stopped and waved cheerily upward and Lara could hear tiny voices calling "Krooom! Krooom!" She released her hold with one hand and waved back at them.

Dominating the city on a low hill near the center was a huge square building with a large dome projecting

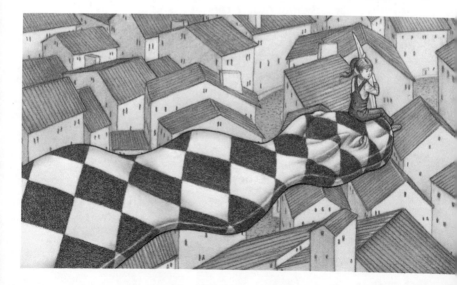

above the roof line. A flagpole was atop the dome and from it fluttered a flag of pure white with a single dark green fir tree in the center.

"That is the palacccce of Mag Namodder," Krooom said, breaking his long silence. "Look in front of the main entry arch. They are awaiting ussss."

Lara looked where he indicated and saw a group of people standing near the large archway in the wall surrounding the palace. A broad, smoothly paved area extended outward from the arch into the city for perhaps a hundred yards. All at once the big snake banked so sharply that she very nearly lost her seat and she gripped his horn with both arms again.

"Pardon me," Krooom apologized. "I sssshould have given you ssssome warning. Hold tight. We're in our final approach pattern now."

He continued banking around at just over rooftop height until they began nearing the paved area from over the city. Then he smoothed out the undulating ripples in his body and glided arrowlike onto the pavement. There was a slithery sliding sound as they touched down and slid with diminishing speed toward the archway. They skidded to a full stop less than a dozen feet from the group of people and immediately Krooom relaxed the flattened muscles and his body resumed its normal shape.

The leader of the group was a tall man with a full white beard but with no other hair on his head. His hands were clasped together across his middle and he was clad in a deep green robe that just touched the ground. The hem, cuffs and collar were white and the sleeves were so large that the cuffs hung nearly to his knees. He smiled broadly, exposing small white teeth, and stepped toward them, raising one of his long-fingered hands in greeting.

"Crobbity," he said, bowing low toward her.

"Crobbity, sir," she replied, dipping in a little curtsy.

"Welcome to the city of Fir Tree," he continued as he straightened. "You are Princess Lara, of course. It was predicted you would come to us at last, but we have waited so many centuries and I had begun to think it would not happen in my lifetime."

"But I am not a princess," Lara protested. "I'm just Lara, Mr. . . ."

"Oh, forgive me, Princess," he said. "I am Menta, leader of the Firtreans and adviser to Mag Namodder. And even though you may not be aware of it, you are indeed a princess and your presence here betokens the fulfillment of the prophecy, assuming we can prevent your being killed."

"Killed?" Lara squeaked. "Why would anyone want to kill me, Mr. Menta? I don't wish anyone harm at all." Her brain was spinning. "What is all this talk of a prophecy I know nothing about and a royal title I know is not mine, but that you say is?"

He shook his head. "It is Mag Namodder's place, not

mine, to tell you of these things. Come. I will take you to her. She is most anxious to greet you." He looked at the snake. "Crobbity, Krooom. You've done very well. You will come with us. Trooom, too, as soon as he arrives."

"My brother will not be coming," Krooom said softly, without explaining.

Menta's brow wrinkled at this but he didn't comment, only turned and led them to the others. The group consisted of a dozen different people. There were two — a man and woman — who looked very much like floppy-eared rabbits, yet who stood erect on their hind legs and were large as kangaroos. They were clad in simple but elegant clothes. Five others — four females and a male — who were obviously huge otters, wore garments similar to the Roman toga and they, too, stood on their hind legs. There were three magnificent hawks who were each slightly taller than Lara, with plumage the color of brushed copper. There was a slight, long-legged, web-footed, froglike individual with huge bulbous eyes and a broad mouth. He wore a short garment of fine chain mail so expertly woven it looked like cloth at first glance. He carried a small round shield on one forearm and there were a dagger and a sword on opposite sides of his belt. Finally, there was a tiny young woman no more than half Lara's height, though obviously quite a few years older, whose immense eyes and waist-length hair were pale green. Though there was no indication how she was able to do so, she hovered a couple of feet off the ground.

These twelve were, Lara was informed, members of the Superior Council, which meant they were the foremost advisers to Mag Namodder. There were a lot of enthusiastic crobbities as Menta introduced them all quickly — so quickly that Lara hardly heard their names — and then hurriedly led them all through the gateless archway and up the wide white steps into the palace.

They passed through an oversized entry room and a sitting room beyond that and then finally into a much larger chamber filled with small round tables. There were four to six chairs at each table. For the first time Lara noted that while many of the guests wore torques, there were at least as many who did not have them. The chamber was thronged with hundreds of people and animals who respectfully stood aside for them to pass. As the new arrivals neared the front of the room, Lara could see a single large chair covered with deep green plush. It was not actually a throne but very close to being one and it was positioned at the head of a large table.

Seated upon the chair was the most breathtakingly beautiful woman that Lara had ever seen. Introduction was not necessary because the little girl knew at once this could be none other than Mag Namodder. She had long dark hair that was braided and piled high atop her head. If Lara had thought about it, she would have guessed the woman's age as being somewhere between thirty and fifty, and she moved with grace as she rose to her feet and came to meet them. As they neared each other, Lara could see that her garment, a one-piece robe belted at the waist, was fashioned of specially softened and intricately woven fir needles and it whispered musically as she moved. The woman held out her hands and grasped both of Lara's; her smile was lovely beyond description.

"Ah, Lara, my dearest little one. You've come back to us again. During these many centuries that have passed there were those among us who feared you were dead and would never return, but I could not — would not! — believe this." Her voice was as delicate and pure as the clear notes of a harp. "Welcome home, my child. Come, sit by me. I know you must be confused by all that has happened and have many things to ask. We will eat first and then I will answer all your questions."

She raised her hand toward the assemblage and made a palm-down motion. Immediately everyone sat down at the tables. The table in front was larger than the others, with room for fifteen people, and this was where Mag Namodder led them and indicated they sit. As directed, Lara seated herself beside Mag Namodder. Menta and the other members of the Superior Council took their seats around the table. There was a special broad table next to this for Krooom, where he had plenty of room to coil himself and both drink and eat by simply leaning his head over to the vessels and containers provided for him.

With another motion and a briefly uttered phrase that Lara could not understand, Mag Namodder caused a splendid tray of food to appear on each of the tables; plump fruits and vegetables that she had never seen before but which in some ways resembled apples, pears, grapes and figs, and fine firm carrots and celery and lettuce and beets and squash. There were also pitchers filled to the brim with liquids that looked like grape juice and apple cider and tomato juice and peach nectar. Yet, much as they resembled familiar fruits and vegetables and beverages, they all tasted much different, unlike anything Lara had ever eaten or drunk before. Most peculiar of all were the vegetables called *metta-metta,* which looked something like an eggplant in size and shape but which were of various dark colors — dark red, dark blue, dark green and dark brown. When sliced, each had a single seed about the size of a Ping-Pong ball and, depending on what color it was, the vegetable tasted like roast beef or boiled ham or leg of lamb or roast pork.

Despite her fascination with the food, Lara was a little irked at stopping to eat at a time like this. She thought herself much too excited to be hungry. However, as she began to nibble at the food she found she was ravenous and she ate and ate and drank and drank until she could hold no more and her stomach had become round and firm. Finally, everyone was finished and Mag Namodder, with another wave of her hand and softly murmured incantation, made all the trays and dishes and mugs and pitchers and remaining food and drink disappear. Lara thought it was the most marvelous way of clearing the table and doing the dishes that she had ever seen.

Mag Namodder now looked at where Krooom was seated and at the large empty place beside him and she became concerned. "And where is Trooom?" she asked.

A sort of shudder went through Krooom, who had eaten nothing, and he wagged his head back and forth sadly. "My brother will be with us no more. He has been killed."

A universal gasping filled the room, followed by a stunned silence. When Krooom did not elaborate, Lara thought she should probably do so.

"If you please, Your Highness," she said, addressing Mag Namodder, "I will explain. Trooom and I were talking together at the great tree when Tark and two other Centaurs came looking for me. There was a big fight. They shot Trooom full of arrows and attacked him with their swords. He killed them, but he was also killed." Her chin was quivering as she finished and tears spilled from her eyes.

Mag Namodder was deeply affected and for a moment she did not speak. When her voice came again, it was soft and very sad and the words were directed at Krooom.

"You have the heartfelt sympathy of us all. Though not so deeply as you, Krooom, we all share your great sorrow. While it can do nothing to bring him back, I will have a fine statue of him erected in the garden before the palace, that the memory of him will always remain fresh in our hearts and minds. And we will do all possible to make sure that he did not die in vain."

"Princess," she said, turning and addressing Lara, "this has been a sad manner of homecoming for you, but the actions of Thorkin and his subjects make it clear that we must move rapidly to save ourselves. Obviously, there are many questions you would like to ask. What would you like to know first?"

Lara was as filled with questions as she was with food and drink, but she had no difficulty asking the one question that was most important to her at this moment.

"Are Barnaby and William safe and unharmed?"

Without meaning to do so, she had innocently asked the one question that Mag Namodder was unable to answer. Lara was immediately dismayed when the beautiful woman's kindly smile faded and a worried little frown caused wrinkles to appear on her brow.

14

The Prophecy

"MY CHILD," Mag Namodder said softly, reaching out and caressing Lara's hair, "I cannot give you a certain answer to that. Boggle came to us with the news of your arrival, which allowed us to send Trooom and Krooom to help bring you here. The other two children have been taken to Castle Thorkin. I can only say that in my heart I know Prince Barnaby and your cousin, William, are still alive. King Thorkin would not risk killing them if he could not kill you at the same time."

"But why should he wish to kill us at all?" protested Lara. "We've done nothing to hurt him. And why wouldn't he kill us if he couldn't kill all three at once?"

"Why, Princess," said Mag Namodder, somewhat surprised at the question, "because of the prophecy."

"Well for goodness sakes," Lara said, a little more sharply than she had intended, "what *is* this prophecy that everyone keeps talking about?"

"Oh, dear," said Mag Namodder, "it never dawned on me that someone hadn't told you by now. Of course you wouldn't know unless they had. I'm sorry. It is a prophecy known to all since earliest childhood. Here in Twilandia, mothers sing it to their daughters and fathers to their sons. And they do so as well in Upperland, though in secret, since it is against Thorkin's edict to say the words. It is written in many places, but inscribed most importantly on the wall of the great room in Castle Thorkin. In this way it is a constant reminder and threat to the King."

"But if it's on the wall in his castle and bothers him so," Lara said, temporarily diverted, "why doesn't he just have it removed?"

"He has tried, Princess Lara." It was Menta who spoke up. "But he cannot."

"He cannot!" echoed the members of the Superior

Council triumphantly. "He has tried, but he cannot."

"He has tried to have it washed off," put in Kreee, one of the beautiful brushed-copper hawks, "but it will not wash."

"He has tried to have it chipped away with chisels," said Slythe, one of the huge otters, shaking his head, "but as soon as the inscription is chipped away, it reappears, inscribed even more deeply."

"He has tried to burn it away with fire," said Billingsworth, the larger of the two floppy-eared rabbit people, who were called Chumplers, "but this only turns the wall black and makes the inscription stand out more legibly."

"He has tried to eat it away with acid," said Rana Pipian, the warrior frog, "but it only makes the letters of the inscription glow."

"He and his chief sorcerer, Warp, have tried to destroy it with terrible spells," spoke up Silkyn, the tiny young woman, who was hovering in a sitting position a foot above the seat of her chair. The Fairy shook her head and her fine hair fluffed in a pale green mist about her head and shoulders. "But even *that* could not make the inscription disappear."

Mag Namodder held up her hand in a gentle gesture and instantly everyone at the table fell silent. She nodded. "All those things are true," she said, "and Thorkin begrudgingly accepts the fact that only one of two things can remove the inscription, so he has had heavy black cloth hung in front of it and it is forbidden under penalty of death even to look toward the cloth."

"You said only one of two things can remove the inscription," Lara said. "What are those two things?"

"That the twins spoken of in the prophecy be killed or that they destroy the King," replied Mag Namodder. "It is Thorkin's greatest fear. That is why, all throughout his reign, it has been his law, whenever twins have been born, that they and their relatives be brought to him that he may put them to death by his own hand, simultaneously."

"All this makes my head spin," Lara said. "And I *still* don't know what the prophecy says."

"You shall hear it now," said Mag Namodder, rising.

"The prophecy!" cried the Superior Council, coming to their feet as one, except for Silkyn, who hovered over the group.

"The prophecy!" cried Krooom, who lifted his upper body so high it was like a great diamond-patterned pillar reaching almost to the high ceiling.

"The prophecy!" echoed all in attendance, and momentarily there was a noisy scraping of chairs as they all came to their feet.

Mag Namodder nodded at Silkyn and the Fairy rose to a point about ten feet above the head table and hovered there. She raised one hand and at once a flood of stirring music filled the great chamber. It was a lively beat and she gave the cue in a reedy voice that carried well across the chamber:

". . . five . . . six . . . seven . . . *Hit it!*"

Instantly hundreds of voices were lifted in a great chorus that was a stirring anthem. Even as they sang the words, Lara was aware that deep inside, somehow she knew them too.

"Three will come together, related by blood,
With two of coincident birth.
These twins will cause problems to rise in a flood
For the King who knows well of their worth.
The throne where he sits is rightfully hers,
With her brother, the Prince, at her side,
These three are they who will vanquish the foe,
Unless by his hand they have died.
Unless by his hand at one stroke they have died,
Unless they are slain with one blow,
They will wrest from his grasp his kingdom so wide
And be honored wherever they go.
Only the weapon she brings to the fore
Can destroy the malevolent King,
And to all of her people their freedom restore
And make every heart leap and sing."

There were cheers and loud cries as they finished and all resumed their seats, respectful silence settling as they listened for what would be said next at Mag Namodder's table.

"You see, Princess Lara," said Menta, "by the words of the prophecy, you are indeed the one who should rule Mesmeria in the place of the evil King Thorkin."

"Yes," added Billingsworth the Chumpler, floppy ears bouncing with his excitement, "with your brother at your side."

"And your cousin, too," put in Whispin, the otter. She was the wife of Slythe.

Lara shook her head. "But you don't understand," she said, a little exasperated, "I'm *not* a princess. I'm just an ordinary little girl from Chicago, who just wants to get my brother and my cousin out of trouble so we can go home."

Now it was Mag Namodder who shook her head and she reached out and touched Lara's arm, her hand cool and smooth and yet filling Lara with warmth and a sense of peace and happiness.

"I am one of the few who knew you when you were just a baby," she said softly. "I was there when Enna, your mother, fled from Thorkin with nothing but you and Barnaby tucked under her arms. Because of spells Thorkin had cast, I was temporarily unable to help, other than to see that she reached the Twilandia turnstile safely."

Already Lara was brimming with questions and comments and they bubbled from her in a stream. "But my mother's name is Anne and she is from Chicago. Even if it was her, why would she have to flee with Barnaby and me? And why would she never have told Barnaby and me about it, and about this place? You say there's a turnstile here in Twilandia, too? Where is it? Can we rescue Barnaby and William and go to that turnstile? What —"

Mag Namodder held up a hand, stopping her. "Enna turned backwards is Anne," she said. "Perhaps she thought the name Anne to be more acceptable in this land called Chicago, of which you speak. Perhaps she did not tell you and Barnaby because she felt you were not yet old enough to be troubled with such concerns. Whatever the reasons, it is of little consequence. You are indeed your mother's daughter. You look exactly like her when she was your age, but when she left here she was eighteen, which is considerably more than twice your age."

"But I have a picture of her!" Lara exclaimed. "Look!" She reached into the pocket of her bib coveralls and took out the compact at the end of the scarlet cord. She snapped it open to the compartment containing her mother's picture and held it for Mag Namodder to see. Instantly, tears rushed to the beautiful woman's eyes.

"Ohhh," she murmured, "it *is* Enna!" She dabbed at the corners of her eyes with her napkin. "There is no doubt of it. And you and your brother are her now much more grown-up little children; no longer the little babes named Lara and Barnaby whom she carried when she fled through the turnstile."

A great confusion roiled Lara's mind. "I'm so confused," she said, her eyes brimming with tears, though she didn't understand why.

Mag Namodder nodded sympathetically. "I see that I must tell you now what your mother could not or would not. You are here and in danger so there is no use in not explaining. You see, your father, Beyon, was King of Mesmeria. He was a very good man, strong and just, and his people loved him very much. They rejoiced when he married Enna and made her his Queen. But King Beyon had a younger brother who hated him because *he* wished to be King. This was not possible unless King Beyon died. Then, when Queen Enna gave birth to twins — first you, Lara, and then a few minutes later, Barnaby — it made the throne even more out of grasp of the King's brother. If King Beyon died, then you, Lara, as his firstborn, would become ruler and, after you, Barnaby."

Lara's eyes had grown big and round and her voice was hardly more than a whisper. "The King's brother . . . was it Thorkin?"

Mag Namodder nodded again. "Yes, child, it was. King Thorkin is your uncle. As the evil Prince Thorkin, he conspired with a sorcerer named Warp and together they planned to slay the whole family — King Beyon,

Queen Enna and the infant Princess and Prince, Lara and Barnaby. Now Thorkin himself had a son. The boy was only eight at the time, but he adored the King and greatly feared his own father, who treated him very badly. The boy overheard Thorkin and Warp making their final plans and though it was a terribly dangerous thing for him to do, he tried to warn the Royal Family. He found Queen Enna and told her, but before they could get to King Beyon, Thorkin and Warp, pretending friendship, approached him and embraced him and renewed their vows of undying loyalty to him, and they followed this by plunging their knives into him and killing him. Then they cut off his head to be sure he was dead and fed his body to a cage filled with Vulpines that had been captured in Dymzonia."

Mag Namodder sighed sorrowfully. "At that point Queen Enna had no choice but to flee with her babies, for she knew Thorkin would try to kill them, too. She came to me. Though I wanted very much to help her, my own powers had been temporarily curtailed by a powerful spell that Thorkin and Warp, working together, had cast upon me. It took great energy for them to cast that spell and it would last for only a few days, so I urged her to let me hide her until then. In the meanwhile I told her I would try to get the Mesmerians to rise to her defense. But Enna was fearful that in just those few days Thorkin and Warp would find them and her babies would be slain. And so she chose to flee through the Twilandia turnstile into the Other World, beyond their reach."

Lara was crying now, thinking of what a terrible time it must have been for her mother; thinking as well with great sadness that she would never get to know her real father. Mag Namodder put her arm around Lara and hugged her close, softly saying "There there," and "Now now," and "Hush hush," until finally the tears stopped and Lara dried her eyes and wiped her nose on her sleeve.

It was Menta who now spoke as Mag Namodder continued to comfort the little girl. His gaze was somber as he told of the many bad things that happened in the world after that.

"Thorkin proclaimed himself King at once and there was none who could dispute him. It did not take him long to learn that Queen Enna had escaped through one of the turnstiles into the Other World, though he didn't know which one. His first act as King was to send a search party through the nearest turnstile, which was the one you came through, Princess, in Verdancia. They were to track down your mother in the Other World and bring her and the two babies — one of which was you, Lara — back to Castle Thorkin, or else to kill you. The search party was comprised of eight people — two Dwarfs, two Fauns, two Tworps and two Centaurs — and it met great peril. Only two returned — a Tworp and a Faun — who told of the horrors of the Other World. On the other side of the turnstile they had found a terrible swamp world. The other six of their party had been killed, five of them by huge dark swimming creatures having great jaws filled with terrible teeth. These creatures grabbed them and dragged them under dark water and ate them. The other one was bitten by a serpent much smaller than Krooom, but the bite was poisonous and he died in terrible agony. So only the two returned and Thorkin, though not satisfied, hoped that these same awful creatures of the Other World had killed Enna and her children.

"But," Menta added, "because he was not certain of this, Thorkin took further precautions. One of his greatest magical powers is the spell called *Mondu,* by which he can reduce people into bare skulls. Anyone he considered a threat was placed under this spell and that is why there are so many skulls mounted on pedestals all throughout Mesmeria. It is also why he has come to be known as the skull King. Just in case Queen Enna had escaped death after all, Thorkin ordered a permanent gatekeeper be placed at each of the five known turnstiles in Mesmeria to watch for any attempt at the Queen's return."

As Menta paused, the tiny flutelike voice of Silkyn broke the silence. "It was only a short time after Queen Enna and her babies escaped that the sun suddenly went out and for the first time in its history, Mesmeria was thrown into darkness. Suddenly there was an intense white light, much brighter than the green glow of the sun, and a voice heard by everyone spoke the prophecy. At the same moment it was written, as if by a fiery finger, on the wall of the great room in the Castle and on the wall of every village hall in Rubiglen, Verdancia, Mellafar, Selerdor and Twilandia."

"That is correct," spoke up Kreee. "Thorkin was terrified and angry and he demanded to know who did it, but no one knew. When he was unable to destroy the inscriptions, he ordered them all covered and no one to gaze upon them under pain of death."

"And it was then, as well," Menta resumed speaking, "that he passed his edict which made it mandatory for every living thing in Mesmeria to be fitted with an unremovable iron torque. Thus, if anyone else tried to escape through a turnstile, he or she would die an agonizing death."

"How awful!" Lara said, remembering only too well how the coin in William's pocket had become so hot when he came through the turnstile.

"Yes," Menta agreed, "it was awful. We here in Twilandia refused to be bound in such a way. In those days there was easy access to Twilandia from many hundreds of different places and Twilandia was considered a part of Mesmeria. But we separated ourselves and closed off all passages except a few well-hidden ones kept secret from everyone above except a chosen few."

"And Boggle is one of those few?" Lara asked.

Menta's expression softened and he smiled. "Yes," he said, "indeed he is."

Thinking of the yellow bird reminded Lara of her brother and cousin and once again she felt her eyes begin to burn with hot tears. "But what are we going to do now about Barnaby and William?"

"Almost certainly," Mag Namodder said, her brow slightly furrowed with thought, "Thorkin will now invade Twilandia in an attempt to find you to destroy you and Prince Barnaby and your cousin."

A thought occurred to Lara and she brightened a little. She even smiled a very small smile.

"The prophecy is wrong," she said.

"How so?" asked Mag Namodder.

"It states that '*Three will come together, related by blood,*' but you see, William is not related to Barnaby and me by blood, only by marriage. He is the nephew of my *step*father."

"The prophecy is not wrong, Princess Lara. It does indeed say '*Three will come together, related by blood,*' but it doesn't refer to William. It refers to your blood cousin, who lives in Mesmeria and who is the son of your true uncle, King Thorkin — the boy who warned Queen Enna. And the three of you *will* come together."

Lara swallowed hard. "Who," she asked, "is this cousin I've never met?"

"He is Prince Daw of Rubiglen."

15

Barnaby's Big Bluff

SINCE we've mentioned Prince Daw, perhaps it's time we go back to Castle Thorkin and catch up on what's happened there, since it's very important to our story.

When Barnaby's explosive "*No!*" stunned the entire assemblage in the great room of the castle and at least temporarily prevented King Thorkin from destroying Roo-Too for her insolence, Barnaby himself was very shocked at what he had done. He knew, too, that he was in extreme danger and his only hope was to try to bluff it through.

Those people who had been standing relatively near the two captives had begun edging away, as if not wanting to be anywhere near them, lest the wrath of King Thorkin include them as well, just because they were close. Even their guards, Blix and his fellow Centaur, moved away from them a little, looking rather apprehensive.

Roo-Too, who had been on the thin edge of disaster only an instant before, stared at Barnaby and her shock diminished. The deep blue eyes suddenly glowed with appreciation and a small smile touched her lips. She dipped her head faintly at Barnaby, the movement sending a little ripple down the length of the long red hair which looked so peculiarly attractive against her pale blue skin.

Prince Daw's mouth was still locked open in a surprised O and he seemed to have lost some of his color. Barnaby couldn't read the expression on his face but he did notice that the young Prince's hand was now resting on the haft of the dagger at his belt.

The magician-adviser, Warp, had leaped to his feet, furious, his heavy gray eyebrows drawn together in a foreboding cloud over angrily squinted eyes. He seemed on the point of raising his staff and invoking some awful spell, but a glance at the monarch stayed him.

King Thorkin was still standing with his ball-topped iron scepter pointed at Roo-Too. Now he unconsciously lowered it as he stared at the boys. The look on his face was frightening and everyone seemed poised for his fury to descend upon the transgressor.

William felt a strong urge to move a little bit away from Barnaby, point at him and say, "It was him who said it, not me!" but he remained in place and felt ashamed for having even harbored such a thought.

Boggle was fidgeting with concern. Still on William's shoulders, he fluffed his feathers and shook his head and stood first on one foot and then on the other, all the time muttering to Barnaby.

"Oh, my," he said, "you shouldn't have said that. Oh, dear. That's trouble! That's *real* trouble. You're in a heap of trouble, boy. Oh, gosh, what a box of troubles you've opened. There's trouble right here in Castle Thorkin. Such trouble you've never seen. Trouble, boy, trouble! Oh, wow, have you got trouble now. There's never been so much trouble as you're in. You're in so much trouble that —"

"Hush, Boggle!" Barnaby whispered and then, before King Thorkin could recover enough to find his voice, the boy pointed at him and spoke harshly.

"Beware, Thorkin!"

(That alone caused another gasp from the crowd, for who would dare address the King without his title, and so disrespectfully to boot?)

"Do not force me to use my powers with so little reason," Barnaby continued in a loud voice, still pointing at the King and hoping no one would notice how his hand was trembling. "How *dare* you keep us waiting like this while you conduct your piddling business!"

William and Boggle were staring aghast, wholly speechless now, and Prince Daw had allowed the faintest of smiles to tilt his mouth-corners upward. A mixture of emotions flicked across King Thorkin's face, from towering rage to uncertainty, as he hesitated, wondering if this little snip of a boy really did have powers that were dangerous to him. That, of course, was exactly what Barnaby had hoped for. At last the King seemed to relax and he smiled.

"Oh, ho!" he said. "Hah! Ho ho ho, hah hah hah, hee hee hee." Amazingly, he was laughing, but then this is what many people do to mask their real feelings when they are uncertain of how to react.

Taking their cue from the King, the assemblage relaxed and a ripple of laughter spread through the crowd. It increased until the room resounded with laughter that was hoarse or shrill or cackling or deep or gruff or giggly, depending on who it came from. Prince Daw was grinning widely and his hand had fallen away from the handle of his dagger. Only the sorcerer, Warp, remained scowling, finding nothing at all amusing in what was happening here.

"Well now," King Thorkin said at last, "you must be Prince Barnaby." He seemed to have forgotten all about punishing Roo-Too.

"I am Barnaby," Barnaby said with grave dignity, "but I know nothing about being a prince."

"Oh, indeed you are, little man," Thorkin said, his smile fading as he came into better control of himself. "You are Prince Barnaby, son of the fugitive Queen

Enna. You have come here to depose me and there is no way I shall allow you to do that. Powers? What powers?" he sneered. "You have no more powers than a rock on the shore of Green Lake. You annoy me, boy, you and your young friend there. Generally speaking, when people annoy me, I destroy them."

Warp smiled at this. "Yes! Do it, Your Majesty. Kill them! They are a threat to you."

It was at this point that Boggle gambled daringly on Barnaby's bluff. He leaped into flight from William's shoulder, executed a tight circle around the two boys and then arrowed toward the King. Ten feet away from the monarch and at eye level, he hovered, wings beating so rapidly they were little more than a yellow blur.

"Your Majesty," he gasped. "Be careful, *please!* You can't imagine the awful powers he has. Why, I've never seen such powers. He can move mountains! He can blank out the sun. Wow, does he ever have power! You've never seen such power in your life before, Your Mightiness. Why, he has powers he's never even tapped. Spells? He's got more spells than anyone's ever had."

"Get away from me, you stupid yellow bird," the King growled. "I don't believe that guff for one moment. I'll take care of them first, and then you!" He started lifting his scepter and it was then that Boggle took an even more desperate chance. In a murmur that no one but he could hear, he cast a spell from his own limited abilities.

"*Pyrotek!*" he whispered, staring at the monarch's hand.

Instantly King Thorkin jerked and yelled "Ouch!" and dropped his scepter. It fell with a heavy clang to the stone floor at his feet and lay there sizzling with the sudden heat that had made it glow redly. Sparks were shooting off the end as if it were a giant sparkler.

"Oh, *no*, Prince Barnaby!" Boggle yelled. "Don't do anything more to him. He didn't really mean to threaten you!"

William stared at Barnaby in amazement and Barnaby, totally befuddled, stared back at his cousin with a what's-going-on-anyway expression. Their attention went back to the front of the room as Boggle darted toward the King, flew three times around his head and then alighted on his shoulder.

"I think I stopped him, Your Majesty," he gasped, "but it was close! Oh, my, was it ever close! Don't anger him any further. There's no telling what he'd do next. No telling at all!" Abruptly he leaned toward the King's ear and whispered urgently. "Listen, Thorkin, you can kill him all right, but not like this. Use your head. Remember the prophecy. You kill these two now, you're in big trouble. You have to kill all three of them at once, remember? Otherwise you'll lose everything. Three's the number. Not one. Not two. *Three!* You better quit wasting time and get the girl. She's the key to the whole thing, and she's in Twilandia with Mag

Namodder. Don't worry about that Underland Witch. You canceled out her powers once before. You can do it again. You've got to get the girl away from her. Remember the prophecy. Once you get those three children together you can roast them or turn them to stone or burn them. You can chop off their heads or turn them into skulls. You can drown them or hang them or —"

"All right, all right!" Thorkin grumbled. "You've made your point. Now get away from me!"

"Righto, King! I'll get away. Boy oh boy, I'll really get away from you. You've never seen anyone get away as fast as I will. I'll leap into the air and flap my wings and —"

"*Go!*" Thorkin roared.

Boggle flitted off his shoulder and landed on Barnaby's. "All right," he murmured to the boys, "I think I've primed him just enough. Let's see what happens now."

"Warp," King Thorkin said, picking up his scepter, which had finally cooled, then turning to face the chief of WAAS, "how many entries do we know of to Twilandia?"

"Four for sure," replied the sorcerer. "Two that enter on the top ledges and require airborne descent. Two others that have precipice trails leading to ground level. They're all unguarded because they think we don't know of their existence."

"All right then, assemble the army. We are going to invade Twilandia immediately. The Vulpine Corps will fly to the attack from the top ledge entries. The rest will move down the precipice trails. Full armament for the troops. We're going to destroy Mag Namodder for once and for all. And we're going to get the girl and kill the three together who are related by blood."

"But the Forest Witch's powers!" Warp protested, becoming a little pale.

"We canceled them out once before," Thorkin reminded. "You're forgetting the Spell of *Oppila*."

"Yes, your Majesty, but it's dangerous to do that and it takes so much energy. That time it took all our combined powers and we were unable to cast any other spells for days afterward. Do we dare risk that?"

"*Yes, we dare!*" thundered the King. "Are you defying me?"

"Oh, no, no, Your Highness, I wouldn't think of it." Warp became even more pale.

"Then do as I order. We march in an hour."

"Do we take Prince Barnaby and his cousin with us?"

King Thorkin considered this. Abruptly he turned and with such suddenness that everyone present was startled, he raised his scepter and pointed it at William.

"*MONDU!*"

Instantly William turned black, then glowed cherry red. The heat being emanated was such that Barnaby

shrank away and a moan escaped him. His cousin! The heat faded. Black bits flaked away until only the bare bones stood there. Then they collapsed into ash and the boy's skull fell with a thud onto the gray material. The only sounds for a short while were those of Barnaby's sobbing.

Just as suddenly as King Thorkin had turned William into a skull, Prince Daw drew his dagger and lunged toward his father. The monarch detected the movement from the corner of his eye and spun about, parried the descending blade with his scepter and knocked it out of Prince Daw's hand. It clattered to rest on the stone floor some distance away.

Immediately the King pointed his scepter at Prince Daw and shouted, "OSSYFIA!" The Prince of Rubiglen, leaning forward and one hand still partially raised, was paralyzed from the neck down. Almost in the same movement, King Thorkin turned and pointed the scepter at Barnaby and repeated the same spell. Barnaby and Boggle, who was still perched on his shoulder, were both similarly paralyzed.

It had all taken only seconds to happen. The King now pointed the scepter at Roo-Too, who was standing where she had been, staring at him defiantly.

"I was looking forward to a very special end for you," he rasped, "but now I have no time. *MONDU!*"

Just as William had, the pretty Roo-Too blackened, became red hot and then swiftly turned into only a skull on ash.

"Do you take me for a fool?" Thorkin said to Prince Daw, who only blinked his eyes in his frustration at being unable to move. The King went on: "Do you think I have forgotten you are my son and that, as such, you are the blood cousin of this one?" He pointed at Barnaby, then looked back at his son. "I've always wondered about it, but now I know — it was you, wasn't it, who betrayed me? You, who warned Queen Enna so she could flee with her babies? *Answer me!*"

"Yes, Father, it was I." The young man spoke in a voice that indicated he was resigned to his fate, but the anger in him remained. "You have no right to this throne. You took it by treachery and murder. Yes," he added defiantly, "I warned them and I've never regretted it. I only wish I had been able to save King Beyon as well."

King Thorkin slapped his son's face twice, so hard that tears spilled from the youth's eyes. "You never were worthwhile having as a son," he said in a grating voice. "Better you had never been born. Well, I'll think of an especially suitable end for you when we get you and the girl and this one together. Perhaps slow boiling in a pot of oil. We'll see."

He turned away and addressed Warp. "All right, get the army prepared. Appoint a couple of Centaur volunteers to bring these two so-called Princes along. You can tell them it won't be such a hard job; they'll only have to carry them one way." He laughed evilly and strode from the great room through the door by which he had entered, followed by his guards.

In a strident voice, Warp issued orders for the troops to go to their barracks, don full armament and assemble to march in one hour. The Centaurs he selected — again it was Blix and his companion — were to return at that time to gather up Barnaby and Prince Daw and carry them along. Within a few minutes the room was cleared of everyone except the two skulls and the paralyzed Prince Daw, Prince Barnaby and Boggle.

"Oh boy," said Boggle, "have we got troubles now. These are real troubles. Have you ever seen such troubles? They're the worst troubles I've ever seen."

"Boggle," Barnaby said, still sniffling, "do you have

to talk so darned much all the time? I wish you'd just be quiet."

Boggle, with poor grace, clamped his beak closed and looked hurt.

After a moment Barnaby suddenly turned his head and looked at the yellow bird. "Say, just a minute! You have magical powers. You unparalyzed Lara. You made the scepter hot in the King's hand so he had to drop it. So what are you waiting for? Cast a spell and free us so we can escape."

Boggle shook his head. "You don't seem to understand the nature of spells," he said. "They take enormous energy to invoke. It takes a great deal of concentration and is terribly enervating. If you try to do too many in too short a time, it weakens you badly. And if you try to do it when you're weakened that way, it can kill you. That *Pyrotek* spell I cast on Thorkin just about drained me. I don't think I've got much left."

"You've got to try, Boggle," Prince Daw said. "Don't you have enough energy left to free at least *one* of us?"

"Maybe," the yellow bird said dubiously. "I suppose I could try."

He squinched his eyes closed and strained. And then he strained some more. Neither of the Princes felt anything, but all at once Boggle breathed a deep sigh, ruffled his feathers, did a couple of quick knee-bends and then took off.

"You were right!" he chortled. "I did have enough

energy left to free one of us. Me. I'm free. Yessir, I'm really free. Boy oh boy, it's sure great to be free again. I'm tired, but I'm free as a bird."

He was circling higher and higher as he spoke and all at once he shot straight forward and streaked through one of the tall slit windows high up the wall and they heard his diminishing voice coming back to them: "Hot diggity, it's great to be free. . . . Couldn't happen to a nicer guy. . . . Everyone should be free if they've got a chance at it. . . . It's really great to be free . . . free . . . free."

Then even his voice was gone and Prince Daw and Barnaby were alone. They couldn't believe the yellow bird had set himself free and abandoned them like this. And, as Boggle had said, they were in the worst trouble they'd ever seen.

16

Approach of the Enemy

LARA was still in the palace of Mag Namodder learning more of her own and Barnaby's beginnings, and of her father, King Beyon, and her mother, Queen Enna. And also of the tyranny of her uncle, King Thorkin. It was all so strange and new and she found herself wishing again that she and Barnaby and William were back again in Everglades City.

Everyone was talking at once and Lara was becoming more and more confused. Seeing her distress, Mag Namodder raised her hand and immediately everyone became silent.

"We are going too far astray in many matters," she said. "We must concentrate our thoughts on the most immediate problems."

"Such as rescuing Barnaby and William," said Lara immediately.

"Yes," said Menta, stroking his white beard with one

hand and rubbing his bald head with the other. "We must definitely do something about that very quickly. And, as Mag Namodder stated earlier, almost certainly Thorkin will now invade Twilandia in an effort to capture Princess Lara. We must prepare for that without delay."

"If his army does invade," put in a worried Mrs. Billingsworth, reaching up to scratch one of her ears with her foot, "how can we stand against them? We have no real army and no weapons to speak of, apart from a few swords and spears. How can we fight against those awful lizards, the crepuscular Krins, who are armorplated and who have great teeth and terrible claws on every toe and those awful tails like whips that can snap a body's head off from twenty feet away?"

"My wife is justified to be so concerned," added Billingsworth, just as worriedly. "How can we stand against the fierce Vulpines, who can swoop down on us from above? Meaning no offense, Kreee," he said to the large copper-colored hawk, "but you and your fellow Kewprums, powerful though you are, simply are not a match for them."

"That depends," Kreee said mildly, "on how many of them may attack us. If they are not too many, we will give them more than they bargained for, I assure you. And do not overlook the great strength and flying ability of Krooom and his kin." Krooom, at the next table, made a deep hissing sound and dipped his head in appreciation for the compliment. "As I said," Kreee concluded, "the Vulpines, may get more than they bargained for."

"Hear hear!" said the members of the Council in chorus. But then came the musical voice of the Fairy, now hovering about a foot above the table.

"We also must not overlook the worst danger of all," she said, "which is the spells that Thorkin and Warp can cast."

"That is an especially important item, Silkyn," Mag Namodder agreed. "Against either of them alone, I would be able to hold my own, but when they combine their powers, as they did once before, they can nullify mine. Since they will undoubtedly have their army with them, they may not resort to such a drastic effort. If they do not, I may be able to contain them. But if they do, all could be lost."

"Excuse me," spoke up Rana Pipian, the warrior frog who was the head of the Twilandia militia, such as it was. "We seem to be overlooking one very vital part of the prophecy. It was stated, in regard to Princess Lara, that '*Only the weapon she brings to the fore can destroy the malevolent King.*' It seems to me that this means no matter what *we* do, the fate of the matter lies in Lara's hands. May I inquire, Princess, just what is this weapon you have brought with you?"

"Weapon?" At first Lara was perplexed, but then she smiled. "Oh, I know! Here it is." She reached into her pocket and took out the slingshot Barnaby had given her. She held it up for all to see. They looked at it curiously.

"What a strange device," said Whispin, the otter.

"Indeed," put in her husband, Slythe. "What is it, Princess, and how are its powers directed?"

"It's called a slingshot," Lara said. "I'll show you how it works." She looked at the beautiful woman beside her. "That is, I will if you don't mind, Mag Namodder."

"Oh, by all means, show us."

On a windowsill about thirty feet away there was a flowerpot with a fern in it. Lara pointed at it. "May I shoot at that?"

"Shoot?" Mag Namodder repeated, holding a hand to her throat. "Oh my, you mean this device *shoots* something? How distressing. I dislike things that shoot. Somehow they're so unfair to the person who is shot at." She sighed. "Well, I suppose, under the circumstances, we have no choice. Yes, dear, you may shoot at it."

Lara stood up and reached into her pocket and withdrew one of the six marbles. She fitted it into the pouch, took her stance and stretched the rubber to its full length. Then she took careful aim and released. The marble sped through the air, missed the flowerpot by about an inch and disappeared into the gardens beyond.

There was a collective sigh. The Superior Council was signally unimpressed.

"Ooops," said Lara, blushing and fumbling in her pocket again, "I missed. Let me try again."

The second shot was considerably better. The marble struck the flowerpot just off center and it burst into pieces, scattering dirt and fern and causing quite a mess.

"Well," said Rana Pipian, breaking the silence that followed, "it's certainly good for breaking flowerpots."

Lara burst into tears. "How . . . how . . ." she blubbered, ". . . how can something like . . . like *this* . . . defeat King Thorkin and . . . and his army?"

"Oh, don't cry, Princess," said Mag Namodder in a soothing tone, taking the little girl in her arms. "It may not look like much, but the prophecy is not to be taken lightly. Perhaps it will have an effect we simply don't yet understand."

She paused a moment and then spoke more briskly. "Well, we cannot afford delay. Rana Pipian, I know you have already put out a call to the militia from all the Twilandia provinces. They've already begun arriving here, and that is good. We can afford to waste no time. Thorkin's attack may come within the next two or three days."

"You're wrong!" came a voice from outside. "Boy, are you wrong. You couldn't be more wrong. Let me tell you how wrong you are."

With a whoosh and a fluttery sound, a yellow bird sailed into the room, skimming just over the shattered flowerpot and landing on the table. He nodded his head generally at the Council members, smiled warmly at Menta and bowed low to Mag Namodder. Then he winked at Lara.

"Boggle!" she cried. "Oh, it's so good to see you. Are William and Barnaby all right?"

Boggle cleared his throat and then sidestepped the question with a somewhat misleading answer. "Barnaby's just fine," he said. "He was out of the Spell of *Ossyfia* for a while, but then Thorkin invoked it on him again. He also cast new spells on William and Prince Daw. But," he added, hurrying on before she could ask more questions, and turning to face Mag Namodder, "that's not the most urgent news. Thorkin and his army are in motion at this moment. They are coming to invade Twilandia. They will be here in a matter of hours."

"Oh, dear!" gasped Mag Namodder. "So little time to prepare! They have discovered our passages to Twilandia?"

Boggle nodded. "Four of them. I don't know which, only that two are to the ledges and the other two to the precipice trails."

"Quickly, then," Mag Namodder said. "There's not an instant to lose. Kreee — swiftest among us are you and your fellow Kewprums. Gather all of them together that you can find and send them to alert every province. Above and beyond the militia already assembling here, every person who is capable of helping defend our country is to come by the fastest means possible, bringing anything they can find to use as a weapon."

Without a word, Kreee and his two Kewprum companions rose, spread their wings and sped through the garden portal and out of sight.

There was a scramble of activity as others were given their orders and left, Rana Pipian directing them. In only minutes the entire room was cleared except for Mag Namodder, Lara and Boggle. It was the Forest Witch who spoke first.

"Now, as briefly as you can — and without repetitions, Boggle! — tell me exactly what has happened."

And Boggle, with remarkable conciseness, told her everything. He faltered only when he came toward the end of his narration and told her about the spells that had been cast on Barnaby and himself and Prince Daw . . . and how the Spell of *Mondu* had been cast on William.

Lara was so stricken with the news she very nearly became hysterical and it took all the soothing and comforting skill Mag Namodder possessed to calm her. When at last the convulsive sobbing began dying away, the woman kissed Lara's forehead.

"I'm sorry, dear Princess," she said softly, "but there will be many other casualties if we do not act quickly. Boggle will take you to a place where you will be safely hidden. You must stay there until —"

"No!" Lara's single word was nearly a wail. "Excuse me, Mag Namodder," she said, "but I won't hide. I must go with you and help defend Twilandia."

"You mustn't, Princess," Mag Namodder said. "You might be hurt or even killed."

"I *have* to go with you," Lara insisted. When Mag Namodder shook her head, the girl hurried on. "I *must!* Don't you see, the prophecy calls for it. It says '*Only the weapon she brings to the fore*' can destroy King Thorkin."

Mag Namodder's shoulders slumped and she sighed. "Truly," she said, "that is what the prophecy says and it is not for me to cause a hindrance to it. All right, you may go with us to meet the enemy and Boggle will be with you at all times. I will give you a weapon — in addition to the one you have — and you must stay close to me, agreed?"

"Oh, yes!" said Lara.

And in that way, Princess Lara was in the forefront of the mass of people of Twilandia who moved away from Fir Tree an hour or so later, heading toward the base of the great cliff, where dangerously narrow trails led up the face of the precipice. Most of the people were armed only with hoes and rakes and broomsticks and pitchforks, but Lara, moving beside Mag Namodder, had a shield that covered almost her whole body and a sword strapped to her middle that dragged on the ground behind her.

And in her hand was the slingshot.

17

Three Tragedies

THERE WERE at least a dozen trails lead-
ing upward from various places at the base of the great
precipice. With no way of knowing for certain which
ones the enemy would be descending, the ill-equipped
little army of Twilanders milled about at the bottom
and waited.

After conferring with Mag Namodder, Rana Pipian,
as militia commander, called an assembly of the Kewprums. He placed the large brushed-copper hawks under
command of Kreee and sent a squadron of them soaring
aloft to watch the various entries to Twilandia from
Upperland. They were to report instantly when it was
ascertained from which entries the invasion was oc-
curring.

Krooom flattened himself into a broad ribbon and,
under the joint command of Slythe and Whispin, a whole
company of the Lutras — the otter people — climbed

onto his back and sat in a single-file row. Each held onto the person in front of him. Slythe himself, at the head of the line, had a strong grip around Krooom's nose horn. With a great slithering sound, Krooom slid across a level meadow and then sped upward with undulating rhythm. A squad of Lutras would be dropped off at each of the isolated ledges, to try to fend off the Vulpines.

Other companies of defenders assembled at the base of each of the precipice paths. They were ready to converge and move up to attack the invaders, as soon as it was discovered by what route they were descending. Each of these companies was headed by a squad of Chumplers, who would lead the way, since they were very agile and could make great leaps. The only weapons the Chumplers had were their powerful feet, with which they could deliver crushing kicks.

Mag Namodder, Menta, Lara and Boggle sat in the grass beneath a large tree and watched the preparations of the militia. Silkyn floated close by and Rana Pipian was no more than a dozen yards away giving instructions to a group of company commanders. They, in turn, would lead their companies of Lutras and Chumplers, Elves and Men, Fairies and Gnomes and Dwarfs and Fauns and Centaurs to repel the attackers when the time came. There was much nervousness among all and a good bit of fear as well, since their fighting skills were

not especially good and their weapons inadequate. Thus a sense of gloom was settling over everyone.

"Mag Namodder," said Lara, "everyone talks about the great magical powers you have. Isn't there some way you can use them to stop Thorkin's army?"

"Good thought," said Boggle. "Excellent thought. Now there's a brainstorm if anyone ever had one. Why, with your powers, Mag Namodder, you can wipe them out easily. Make them explode. Turn them to stone. Turn them inside out. Change them into bedbugs. Great idea!"

Mag Namodder sighed. "My powers," she said, "are primarily to help people, not harm them. They are for good, not for evil. Yet, in an emergency I can call on certain powers to perhaps nullify the evil magic of others. In this case, if I were able to see Thorkin and Warp before they saw me, I might be able to make them lose their powers for a while. It wouldn't stop them from fighting, but it could stop them from casting dangerous spells on our people."

"Well," Lara persisted, "couldn't you do that now? Before they get here?"

"Absolutely!" Boggle exclaimed, fluffing his feathers and bobbing his head in an excited manner. "Just the thing to do. Nip them in the bud, as it were. Do unto them before they do unto us. Splendid thought!"

"Not really, Boggle," spoke up Menta. He turned to look at the little girl. "Princess Lara, until the attackers leave the rock passageways and come into the open, there would be too much interference. Why, even a light fog or rain can oftentimes cause too much interference. For maximum effect, most spells are cast in relatively close proximity. Now, since it's a good clear day today, if Thorkin and Warp appeared on one of the ledges up there in the open," he pointed toward the top of the cliff, "Mag Namodder could disable them with her spells, at least temporarily. As Mag Namodder has indicated, our only hope is that she will be able to see them in the open before they see her."

Rana Pipian strode up just then and overheard the tail end of the conversation. "As with most army commanders," he put in, "Thorkin and Warp will probably send in their elite forces first to wear us down before they ever expose themselves. Mag Namodder cannot take the chance of wasting her powers on the army. We can only hope to fight them off well enough that their leaders have to expose themselves to direct operations."

"Can . . . can we," said Lara, swallowing, "defeat them?"

Mag Namodder shook her head. "I must be honest with you, Princess," she said. "I don't think we have much of a chance. It's possible but not very likely. All we can do is try our hardest and hope for the best."

At that moment a Kewprum, diving from the highest reaches of the cliff, leveled off and shot toward them in a blur of speed over the meadow. It was Kreee and at the last moment he cupped his wings and, with a loud whooshing sound, settled to the grass near them.

"Rana Pipian," he said hurriedly. "We have spotted two parties of them beginning to emerge at the top of the central precipice trail and the one to the left of that. The main assault seems to be coming down Central Trail. Only two Gnomes have appeared at the first entry to the left of that and we take them to be spies sent forward to make a reconnaissance and report back to their leaders on our strengths and weaknesses."

Rana Pipian nodded. "Excuse me, Mag Namoddder," he said. "I must go and start our people up Central Trail."

Immediately he raced off, Kreee flying beside him, and in a few minutes an advance party of Chumplers began bounding up Central Trail as other ground forces converged to follow them. Soon a whole stream of people were moving upward. Lara thought they looked like nothing so much as a line of ants crawling up the side of a building.

Suddenly there were some loud cries and a sound like the whistling of a bomb approaching them. A Vulpine, wings half-closed, plummeted toward them from far above, with three Kewprums in pursuit. Down and down came the Vulpine, until it seemed sure to crash into the ground. At the base of the cliff it abruptly leveled off and screamed over the heads of the defenders waiting their turn to start up Central Trail.

Though much larger than the three copper-colored hawks in pursuit, the Vulpine made no attempt to turn and engage them in battle. Instead, having sped across the entire force waiting at the foot of the cliff, deftly dodging the scattering of spears, arrows and stones lofted against it, the great greenish-black bird veered and shot toward the small group standing near the tree. Kreee flashed in from an angle, trying to intercept the enemy, but missed by mere inches and took up the pursuit directly behind.

The Vulpine came past Mag Namodder and her group so low and so fast that the grasses were nearly flattened by the wind of its passage, while the leaves of the tree whipped wildly and a few were torn away. As the huge bird passed, its great saucer-like, amber-colored eyes fastened on them for just an instant. Then the bird was gone. It banked sharply to avoid Kreee and the other three Kewprums that were closing in and beat its powerful wings very hard, going into a steep climb.

Up and up it flew, not leveling off until it reached the very top of the cliff. It seemed to be tiring because it slowed as it passed the mouth of the entry where the two Gnomes were standing, observing. Immediately Kreee slashed in to attack, striking the larger bird with his talons and snapping at it with his beak.

Although Kreee caused damage to the Vulpine, it was not enough. The great dark bird did a mid-air somersault, knocking Kreee off its back. Before Kreee could recover his balance, the savage beak of the Vulpine snapped at him and clipped off one of his wings. Kreee shrieked and then plummeted out of control. Everyone watched him fall and then thump heavily to the ground at the base of the cliff, where he lay lifeless. A great cry of despair and anger erupted from the defenders at this terrible tragedy.

The Vulpine was now approaching the Central Trail entry, but the other three Kewprums overtook it before it could get there. They attacked simultaneously, pouncing upon it and tearing at it with talons and beaks. In a moment the Dymzonian bird was itself disabled and falling. It crashed to a ledge of jumbled rocks, bounced away and fell the rest of the way to the ground amidst the cheers of the Twilanders.

On the precipice's Central Trail by this time, the descending Upperland force was just meeting the first advance squad of ascending Chumplers. A fierce battle broke out and, even though far below, the onlookers could hear the faint cries and the sound of metal crashing against metal as swords smashed against pitchforks and hoes or other swords. Soon some of those battling began to fall from the precipice trail — a few of the enemy, but mostly Chumplers and then even Lutras, as the otter people reached the battle site.

A series of wrinkles had appeared on Mag Namodder's brow. "I think," she said slowly, "they may be trying to fool us. The main battle appears to be there on Central Trail, but look, no more of the enemy are emerging from that entry."

It was true. The stream of enemies that had poured out of the tunnel high above onto Central Trail had ceased and now the defenders, swarming up that trail, greatly outnumbered the attackers. A rousing cheer went up from the Twilanders, but it was not echoed by Mag Namodder and her party.

"I believe the main force will be coming out of that tunnel," she went on, pointing at the entry ledge high above them and to the left, where the two Gnomes still stood. "Almost certainly Thorkin and Warp will emerge behind them. Unless . . ."

Her frown deepened as a distressing thought suddenly

struck her. Quickly she raised both her arms toward the ledge where the Gnomes were, but too late. The death of Kreee had been tragedy enough, but now a second tragedy was in the making. A wink of blue light appeared on that ledge. From it a beam of intense light no larger than a pencil shot down and struck her. For a moment she stood transfixed. A blue glow bathed her and she made a low wailing sound. Then the blue light vanished and she crumpled to the grass.

All was turmoil. Lara and Menta and the others rushed to her. A large number of the Twilanders still at the base of the cliff also rushed over and soon there was quite a crowd milling about Mag Namodder. She was breathing and still conscious, but was so dazed she was unable to recognize anyone.

"Oh, my," murmured Menta, who was terribly concerned, "it was this way when Queen Enna was escaping. It's the Spell of *Oppila!*"

Shadows swept across them, accompanied by a rushing of wind, and everyone was yelling or screaming at once. The air had become full of flying forms as scores of Vulpines swooped down upon them, with Kewprums following the Vulpines, attacking them. Everyone on the ground was running around bumping into each other and no one seemed to know what to do. Such turmoil! Hordes of invaders were now descending the trail from the tunnel entry where the Gnomes had been standing.

Leading the way was a battalion of the dreadful crepuscular Krins.

A trio of Vulpines in close formation swept in no more than two or three feet off the ground, the saw-toothed leading edges of their wings cutting a wide swath through the defenders. Behind the three came another, its head moving back and forth as if searching for something, and this was the beginning of the third tragedy. Lara saw them and stood frozen in place, fascinated and fearful. In one corner of her mind she wondered what the one Vulpine was looking for. Then she found out.

Her.

The great dark birds banked sharply and came directly toward her. She dropped both the cumbersome shield and sword and ran as fast as she could for a little distance, then threw herself to the ground. The three birds in formation passed directly over her with a rush. Then the fourth approached and she covered her head with her arms and tried to make herself as small as possible, but it didn't help.

She felt great taloned toes snap down and encircle her like a basket and she was lifted and carried away. To make matters worse, she dropped her slingshot in the struggle. No one even knew she had been caught until her screams reached them from high above, but by then it was too late.

Almost too late.

A small creature launched itself from the ground and, flying faster than it had ever flown before, began to follow the four Vulpines. It was bright yellow and about the size of a chicken.

Boggle.

18

The Affair
on the Precipice

NOW we're going to have to back up just a little and find out about those two Gnomes who had appeared at the mouth of the first tunnel entry to the left of Central Trail.

Just as Mag Namodder had realized — but too late! — they weren't Gnomes at all. There were actually King Thorkin and Warp who had reluctantly used just enough of their power to cast a spell that temporarily gave them the appearance of Gnomes. The only clue to their identity was that Thorkin still had his sword belted to his waist and Warp carried his crooked staff.

Blix and the other Centaur were directly behind them, carrying Prince Daw and Prince Barnaby. Most of the army was in the dark rocky tunnel behind them. They had reached the secret passage only a few miles from Castle Thorkin in the Gray Mountains. Hidden in a large clump of bushes on the mountainside, the opening appeared to be nothing more than a cave. Thorkin sent a couple of companies to the other known precipice trail entry not far distant and then he and Warp led the main force into the cave.

The passage had angled downward a long way and it wasn't until they had been following it for several hours that they saw daylight far ahead. When they reached a point only a few dozen feet from the opening, they stopped. That was when Thorkin and Warp turned themselves into Gnomes. The pair moved out onto the ledge and saw that not only was the detachment beginning to emerge and descend from the tunnel entry some distance to their left, but that the defending Twilanders had assembled at the base of the cliff and some were already beginning to ascend Central Trail to meet those invaders.

"Good, good!" Thorkin said, rubbing his hands together in a very satisfied way. "Soon my Vulpines will be emerging from the ledges without trails. And now, Warp, we have a straight-line shot to cast the Spell of *Oppila* on Mag Namodder."

"Assuming she's down there with them," Warp replied darkly. "She may have gone into hiding with the girl."

"No," said Thorkin, "she wouldn't do that. She's one of those silly kinds of people who wouldn't send her followers into things she wouldn't go into herself. No, she'll be there."

Inside the tunnel, Barnaby and Prince Daw had been propped against the passage wall by the two Centaurs. Blix and his companion, who wanted to take a rest from carrying the two in their arms, were now standing a dozen feet away, their attention on King Thorkin and Warp.

"We've got to do *something*," Barnaby whispered.

"Yes," Prince Daw whispered back, "something. Only I don't know exactly what."

"I wish I had my slingshot," Barnaby lamented, "and was able to move so I could use it. I'd hit the King in the forehead just like David did with Goliath and knock him over the edge."

"What's a slingshot?" Prince Daw hissed. "Who's David? Who's Goliath?"

"Never mind. We can't do anything anyway, long as we're paralyzed from the neck down."

"We'll see about that," Prince Daw said. "I'm not good at spells yet and have only learned a few, but I got a chance to look at Warp's old spell books once when he wasn't around. One of those I saw was the Anti-*Ossyfia* Spell. I only got to read half of it, but I remembered it. I just tried it out."

"Can you move now?" Barnaby asked eagerly.

"More than before, but not all the way. Just half-way — from the waist up. I guess that's because I read only half the spell. It's not much, but it's something and maybe it'll help."

Barnaby was about to reply but an exclamation from King Thorkin silenced them both.

"Drat!" said the King. "We've been spotted."

A beautiful copper-colored hawk of large size was flying past. It looked at the pair on the ledge and then dived sharply toward the Twilanders. At once Thorkin looked back into the darkness of the passage and called loudly, "Urp! Come here!"

One of the five Vulpines with his main army plodded forward, the great taloned feet making heavy scratching noises on the rock floor. He stopped before the King and sorcerer and bowed respectfully.

"Urp," Thorkin said, "drop down there and take a close look. See if you can spot Mag Namodder. You know what she looks like. While you're at it, see if you can see the little girl anywhere. Not likely, but take a look anyway." Recalling what Blix had told him while being questioned on the way here, he added, "She's wearing blue denim bib coveralls. When you come back, don't land here. Just fly past and yell what you've discovered and then go over there," he pointed toward Central Trail, "and help kill those Twilandian fools."

"Aye-aye, Your Majesty." The Vulpine raised one great wing in salute and nearly knocked over Warp, who gave him an angry look. Then he plodded to the rim of the narrow ledge and plunged off.

The ruler and his magician watched the Vulpine as he dropped and they saw three Kewprums take up a pursuit of him when he was halfway down. They continued watching as Urp leveled off near the ground and sped across the army. They saw him veer toward a little knot of people near an isolated tree, then up and away, still being pursued. As the Vulpine neared their ledge, he slowed in order to call to them as he passed.

"They're *both* there, by the tree!"

Urp flew on, but his slowing had allowed a Kewprum to catch up. They grappled and Urp bit off the other bird's wing and it fell. Thorkin and Warp hardly noticed. Their attention was riveted to the isolated tree far below.

"Can we afford one more minor spell?" the King asked.

"Which?" Warp responded.

"*Bynock.*"

Warp considered this and then nodded. "Yes, that we can do, but for no more than a few minutes. Anything beyond that and there won't be energy enough for the Spell of *Oppila.*"

At King Thorkin's nod, Warp raised his hand, fingers outstretched toward the King and muttered a brief incomprehensible phrase. Then he did the same with himself. A shimmering similar to heat waves appeared in the air before the faces of each man and then it was gone. There was no other outward change but now, for a few minutes, each was possessed of telescopic vision. They had no difficulty spotting both Mag Namodder and Princess Lara.

At once the two men who appeared to be Gnomes crossed their wrists and each placed the flat of his palms against the other's. Both strained and strained until blood vessels bulged in their necks and temples and perspiration broke out on their foreheads. Simultaneously they cried, "*OPPILA!*"

A blue light as bright as that from a welder's torch engulfed their hands and a pencil-thin beam of the same light shot down at an angle and struck the tiny figure of Mag Namodder far below. In an instant it was over and the two Gnomes were again Thorkin and Warp, both of them staggering from the vast output of combined energy the Spell of *Oppila* had cost them.

From their right came a swarm of Vulpines to attack the Twilanders climbing Central Trail and those still on the ground below. Immediately King Thorkin shouted to the four Vulpines still with him.

"Retch! Take your three to run interference for you and get that girl, *now!* Bring her back to me, unharmed. Go!"

The four Vulpines conferred briefly and then three launched themselves from the ledge, followed only an instant later by Retch. As soon as they were gone, Thorkin ordered the main army forward and down the narrow precipice trail from this ledge. The order was relayed from one company commander to another, echoing back through the depths of the tunnel.

The crepuscular Krins led the way, their scaly armored bodies slithering over the rocks as they poured from the mouth of the tunnel and started the descent with great agility. A horde of Gnomes armed with spears followed and, after them, a mob of Elves and Dwirgs and Tworps and Dwarfs and Men and Nyads and Satyrs and Centaurs. The army had bows and arrows and shields and swords and spiked maces. They were all shouting loudly and making a terrible din.

By this time the Twilanders recognized the newer and greater danger and were streaming up the narrow trail. The Kewprums, bounding upward most rapidly, attacked the leading Krins when they were about half-way down. It was a terrible battle. The huge brushed-copper hawks flashed in to grip and tear and drag Krins to the edge and force them to plunge to their deaths. The Krins chopped at the attackers with their awful multitoothed mouths. Even worse, they snapped their deadly accurate whip-tails at the birds with cracks like gunfire, causing the birds to burst in a shower of metallic feathers as they fell to their deaths.

Warp and King Thorkin were among the last to start the descent, followed by Blix and his companion Centaur carrying Barnaby and Prince Daw. They didn't get very far. As they reached a slightly wider place in the treacherous descent, Retch, carrying Lara in the basket formed of his talons, sailed into view. He flapped mightily and hovered a few feet over the trail ahead of them, then dropped the girl with a plop and flew off to join in the battle.

Lara grunted and then scrambled to her feet, limping slightly from a scraped knee. She barely glanced at Thorkin and Warp and Prince Daw and the Centaurs before her gaze fastened on her twin brother.

"Barnaby!" she cried and ran toward him.

"Not so fast," King Thorkin growled, snatching her as she tried to run past him.

Lara kicked at his shins and flailed ineffectively with her fists at his middle.

"At last! The *three together related by blood* are in my power!" He laughed loudly in a nasty way and glanced at the Centaurs.

"Set them down," he ordered, "and go help fight the battle. Your job with these two is over."

Blix and his companion did as ordered, setting the pair on their feet, then clattering off down the trail. King Thorkin shoved Lara at the sorcerer.

"Hold her, Warp. It's time for the executions." He laughed horribly. "I've waited centuries for this."

Warp gripped Lara roughly and Lara struggled until he pinched her so hard it brought tears to her eyes and she had to stand still to make him stop. Her eyes widened as King Thorkin drew his large black-bladed sword and advanced on Prince Daw. "You first," he grated. "Beheading is the reward for betraying your own father."

"No!" Barnaby cried. "Don't do it."

"Stop!" Lara cried. "He's your own flesh and blood!"

Ignoring the children, the King stopped before the young Prince and then, without another word, swung the sword in a vicious arc at his neck.

Summoning all his energy, Prince Daw bent down sharply from the waist and the blade whooshed harmlessly over his head. Thorkin was astonished, since he believed his son to be paralyzed under the Spell of *Ossyfia*. Before he could recover to strike again, Boggle flew into the scene, chattering a rapid-fire monologue.

"I'm here! To the rescue! Yessir, I'm here, I am! All's well. Not to worry — Boggle's here!"

He landed hard atop King Thorkin's head and grasped the King's hair with his feet to hang on. His wings flapped in harsh blows to the sides of the monarch's head. At the same time he leaned down and began pecking furiously toward the King's eyes.

Thorkin dropped the heavy sword with a clatter and started reaching up with both hands to tear Boggle off his head. Again Prince Daw leaned forward, so much that he went off balance and began to fall, but he was still able to grip his father around the chest, pinning the big man's arms to his sides. All the while, Boggle continued pecking and pecking, ranting at him continuously.

"Take *that*, you craven King! And *that*, you wretched

wretch! And *this,* you terrible tyrant! And *this* you mon-
archial monster! And . . ."

Under normal conditions, Thorkin would merely have
thrown off both his son and Boggle without any difficulty, but he was still very weak from invoking the Spell
of *Oppila* on Mag Namodder and though he shook his
head savagely and thrashed about, dragging Prince Daw
with him, he couldn't immediately shake off the bird or
break his son's grip.

"Help me, Warp! Kill this blasted bird!"

Warp released Lara, tossed his staff aside and snatched
up Thorkin's fallen sword. He swung it hard at Boggle,
but the yellow bird saw it coming and leaped straight
into the air, so the blade passed just beneath his feet
and just over Thorkin's head. Expecting the heavy sword

to be checked somewhat by contact with the bird and unaccustomed to its heavy weight, Warp was thrown off balance when the sword cut through nothing but air. Its weight pulled him to one side and he teetered on the rim of the trail for an instant and then fell.

"*Ornitha! ORNITHA!*" the sorcerer shrieked, trying to call up the spell that would give him the power of flight. But his spell power had all been used up for now and he fell screaming, arms and legs thrashing and Thorkin's sword tumbling through the air beside him. Seconds later, when he struck the rocks at the bottom, the ground heaved and roared as if with a minor earthquake.

Warp was no more.

The effects were felt immediately. The battle continued, but the attackers seemed suddenly less sure of themselves and they faltered. Not far away, Mag Namodder blinked rapidly several times and smiled at Menta and Silkyn, who were tending her. She seemed to be coming back to her senses.

On the high precipice trail, however, matters remained desperate. King Thorkin threw Prince Daw to the ledge and though the young man tried to pull himself along with his hands and arms, he wasn't very successful. Boggle was flapping in one place about a foot above Thorkin's head.

Lara saw Warp's discarded staff and she ran to snatch it up, but the King intercepted her. He knocked her away with a backhand blow and grabbed up the staff himself. He swung it unexpectedly and hit the hovering Boggle solidly. In a cloud of feathers, the yellow bird tumbled through the air, hit the cliff and fell in an unmoving heap on the precipice trail. Thorkin laughed aloud and then turned to face his niece and nephew and son.

"If I can't *cut* your heads off, I'll smash them," he growled.

Lara had been knocked over and landed on the marbles still in her pocket, which made her wince. But, reminded of their presence, she reached into her pocket for them. If nothing else, she could at least throw them at the King. She was too slow. Seeing her movement, Thorkin lunged at her and clasped her wrist. Then he pulled her hand from her pocket and squeezed until the pain made her open her clenched hand. In her palm there were four marbles.

Thorkin seemed afraid to touch them. Still gripping her wrist with one hand, he dropped the staff, picked her up about the waist and carried her to the rim of the trail. "Drop them," he ordered, "or I'll drop you."

Fearful of the dizzying drop directly beneath her, she obeyed, and the four marbles fell out of sight below.

"Now, let's see what other tricks you've got in your pockets," he said.

He patted them in turn, finding them empty until he reached the bib pocket of the coveralls. Carefully, he reached in and withdrew the gold-colored plastic compact attached to her pocket by the scarlet cord. Unable to see it closely enough, he jerked it sharply and her pocket ripped as he tore it away. He looked it over suspiciously, shook it near his ear and then looked at it again.

"What's inside this?" he demanded. "Answer me!"

"Just . . . just a picture of my mother," Lara sniffled.

Thorkin remained suspicious. "You think I'm going to believe that?" He walked with her and the compact over to Barnaby and set her down. Then he gripped her paralyzed twin's throat so roughly that Barnaby's breath immediately began rasping. With his other hand, he extended the compact toward Lara.

"Open it," he ordered. "Slowly and carefully. If there's any suggestion of its being a weapon, I'll break your brother's neck before you have a chance to use it."

"Please, don't hurt Barnaby," Lara said. "It's just a compact, not a weapon. See."

She touched the catch and it opened to the compartment with the small framed picture of her mother.

"All right," Thorkin said, relaxing a little, "let me see it." He held out his hand for him to give it to her.

Lara snapped it shut and handed it to him. King Thorkin took it and pressed his thumb to the catch. The compact popped open and Thorkin looked inside. Instantly his face became contorted. His eyes bulged and his lips curled away from gnashing teeth. A deep,

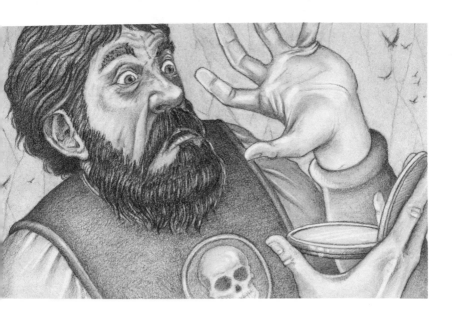

agonized cry erupted from his mouth. Then his eyes
rolled upward and he collapsed.

Prince Daw looked at Barnaby and then at Lara.

Barnaby looked at Prince Daw and then at Lara.

Lara looked at Barnaby and Prince Daw and then at
Thorkin.

"What happened?" Barnaby croaked, his throat still
hurting from the King's grip.

"I don't know," Lara replied, shaking her head. She
approached the fallen King slowly and took the compact
out of his relaxed hand and slipped it into her pocket.
Then she reached out gingerly and placed three fingers
on his wrist, as Mother had shown her how to do, and
tried to feel his pulse. There was no pulse to feel.

King Thorkin was dead.

1 9

The Weapon Revealed

THERE WAS still a little sporadic fighting after the death of King Thorkin, but not much, and it didn't last for long. And in every case, those instances of fighting occurred where the defenders still had a chance to grapple with the attackers, most of whom were suddenly fleeing.

The forces that had been under Thorkin's rule suddenly felt a freeing of their spirits. They had for so long been under his control that they hardly realized they had almost no free will of their own. The sudden freeing of their spirits was an overwhelming joy for most and, though they retreated, no army had ever before retreated with such a feeling of relief and delight.

The voracious Vulpines were first to disappear. With powerful wingbeats they sped through the air, back to the tunnel ledges where they had entered Twilandia. Small forces of Lutras left on those ledges by Krooom stood aside and watched the Vulpines land and scramble as rapidly as they could into the dark tunnels. The huge greenish black birds were no longer making any attempt to fight. They wanted only the opportunity to get back to the surface of Upperland where they could take wing and fly back to Dymzonia. The otter people, realizing this, simply stood back and watched them go.

The crepuscular Krins were next to leave, their reptilian bodies slithering rapidly back up the narrow precipice paths they had descended and disappearing into the tunnel mouths. They, too, had no further desire to fight here, especially since many had lost their sunglasses in the fighting, and they wanted only to return to their own portion of Dymzonia where they could continue to war with the Vulpines and be ready to attack anyone who entered their land.

As for the remainder of the attackers — the Gnomes and Centaurs, the Tworps and Dwirgs and Men and Fauns and Satyrs and others — they not only lost all desire to fight, but they found themselves suddenly reunited with old friends who had many years ago fled from Upperland and taken refuge in Twilandia from the tyranny of King Thorkin. There were many hugs and kisses and handshakes and backslappings. There were cheers and hurrahs and laughter and tears of joy. Mag Namodder proclaimed that hereafter the anniversary of this date would be celebrated as a national holiday and that it would be called Lara Day, which would be something like a combination of Christmas and the Fourth of July.

On the ledge where Lara and Barnaby and Prince Daw and Boggle were, as soon as King Thorkin died, his remains began to diminish. Smaller and smaller they became until they were the size of a little doll and then even smaller until no larger than a peanut. Then they shrank even more until only the size of a dust mote — a tiny fragment which suddenly blew away on a little gust of breeze. And Lara felt a chill run through her because at that moment she thought she heard the tiniest of voices shrieking angrily, "I'll be back . . . back . . . back . . ." but then it faded away and she decided it had been no more than the whispering of the breeze.

The two boys suddenly found themselves free of the Spell of *Ossyfia*. Barnaby rushed to Lara and they embraced and even cried a little together because they were so happy. Barnaby introduced his twin to Prince Daw and Lara kissed her older cousin on the cheek and he hugged her in a very proper manner and it was all a very wonderful time.

Boggle, who sat up groaning only a moment after that, was gathered up tenderly by Lara and found to have a broken wing. He wanted to know what had happened to King Thorkin and the war and why everything looked brighter and nicer than before. All three children began talking excitedly and Boggle finally sorted out what had transpired, although no one was sure at all why King Thorkin had collapsed. When they were finished, Boggle reacted in typical Boggle manner.

"Oh, how wonderful! Ouch, my wing hurts! What a terrific day! Oh, the pain! What a marvelous end to things. Wow, that wing really smarts! Isn't this a tremendous event? Oooh, my aching wing!"

That went on and on, with no one caring at all how much Boggle talked, until suddenly there was a great sliding whoosh of a sound as Krooom landed on the narrow path with great skill and bowed his head toward them with the deepest of respect.

"Sssso glad to ssssee you are ssssafe, Princess Lara. And you, Princcccce Daw. And you, Princcccce Barnaby. We were all disssstressssed at the posssssibility that King Thorkin had harmed you. Mag Namodder hassss ssssent me to bring you back to the palacccce in Fir Tree, where a great victory banquet issss to be held in your honor. Pleasssse, climb aboard."

And so, with Lara cradling the still-talking Boggle in one arm and holding onto Krooom's nose horn with the other, and with Barnaby seated behind her, his arms about her waist, and with Prince Daw behind him, his arms about Barnaby's waist, they left the dangerous ledge. Krooom flattened his body and launched himself into the air and they sailed in that wonderfully exhilarating way to the smooth landing strip before Mag Namodder's palace at Fir Tree.

Menta was there, as was Silkyn, floating close to his shoulder. Mr. and Mrs. Billingsworth, the Chumplers, were there, both with bandages over minor wounds. Rana Pipian was there, walking with the aid of a make-shift crutch, since he had suffered an arrow wound in his ankle, but he was smiling and otherwise unhurt. Both Slythe and Whispin were there, unharmed and wreathed with smiles at the reunion. And, of course, Mag Namodder was there as well and it was she who approached with outstretched arms to be first to greet them. She hugged and kissed them all — although being very careful with Boggle because of his wing. Menta, who was a very good doctor, quickly set Boggle's broken bone and put a splint on the wing. Boggle was very brave about it and only said ouch about a dozen times, which was really not very much at all for Boggle.

As soon as Menta was finished ministering to the yellow bird, Mag Namodder conferred in whispered tones with Boggle and then placed him on Krooom's snout and whispered to the giant snake as well. Krooom and Boggle listened carefully and then dipped their heads respectfully. As Mag Namodder stepped back, Krooom once more flattened himself and, with Boggle using his uninjured wing to hang on tightly to the snake's nose horn, took off with a rush and flew away toward the clifftop tunnel.

After they were gone from sight, Mag Namodder led everyone into the palace. Hundreds of tables had been set up in the great banquet hall and were heaped with wonderful things to eat and drink. All who were present took their places, with Lara, Barnaby and Prince Daw at the head table with Mag Namodder and the Superior Council.

"There are many things we must discuss," Mag Namodder said, loudly enough for all to hear, "but first we will refresh ourselves with the food and drink at hand. For those of you who have become exhausted from the fighting or who have suffered cuts or scratches or bumps, some of the food has healing capabilities and you will find your pain disappearing and the wounds well on the way to being completely cured by the time you have finished. For the time being, then, let us eat and rejoice in our victory."

Loud hurrahs from the crowd followed her words and soon the great room became somewhat noisy with the jangling of forks and spoons and even noisier with conversations at every table as individuals told of their own activities during the battle and of the incidents of heroism they had witnessed.

At the head table, Mag Namodder asked to see Lara's compact, having ascertained that this was evidently the device referred to in the prophecy as being *the weapon she brings to the fore.* Lara handed it to the Forest Witch, who opened it and inspected the compartments carefully. She nodded and murmured, "So that was it," then snapped it closed and handed it back to the little girl.

Lara slipped it back into her pocket, but she was very puzzled. "Excuse me, Mag Namodder, but I don't understand. How could King Thorkin be destroyed just by looking at a picture of my mother?"

"It was not the picture of Queen Enna that destroyed him, child," said Mag Namodder. "You snapped the compact shut before handing it to him. When he pushed the snap, he pushed not the one that opened to the picture compartment, but rather the one that opened to the other compartment. As you have no doubt noticed, there are no reflections in this world. Even water does not reflect images. When Thorkin mistakenly opened the compact to the mirror compartment, he was able for the first time in his life to see himself as others saw him. Most people never experience this. People have a way of justifying in their own minds whatever they do, no matter how bad it might be. But a good mirror reflects only a true image. The mirror in your compact reflected the terrible evil in Thorkin's eyes and his eyes reflected the terrible evil that has lodged for so long in his heart. It was so awful that even he could not bear it and the magical power for evil that was inside him rose up and destroyed him."

Among those who overheard her, there were some who were very anxious to see this strange thing called a mirror, but, sad to say, there were many others who were afraid to look into it for fear of what they would see. Nevertheless, there was a roar of approval when

Mag Namodder suggested the compact be enshrined as a Freedom Memorial for viewing by all who cared to see it, provided Princess Lara agreed.

Princess Lara agreed.

There was general conversation at the head table after that, as everyone joined in the banquet. Lara and Barnaby whispered to one another, however, and only picked at their food a little and they didn't smile and laugh as the others were doing. In fact, Mag Namodder suddenly noticed that there were tears running down Lara's cheeks and dripping off her chin. Immediately she rose and kneeled beside the girl and took her in her arms. She smoothed Lara's hair back and dabbed at her tears with a soft napkin.

"There, there, dear," she soothed. "Tears at such a time? What's the matter?"

Lara was by this time sniffling so much she had trouble speaking. "It's . . . it's . . . it's *William*. How can Barnaby and I ever explain to Uncle Danny and Auntie Alice that he's been turned into a . . . a . . . skull?"

The faintest hint of a smile turned up the corners of Mag Namodder's lips and made little crinkles at the corners of her eyes. Before she could respond, however, they heard sounds of muted cheering from outside and then a slithery sound approaching in the adjoining halls. Abruptly the great doors were thrown open and a familiar voice became clear.

"We're back everyone! We're back! We've been to

Castle Thorkin, but we're back now. We're really back. And do we have a surprise for you! A terrific surprise. Such a surprise you've probably never had. An absolutely wonderful, glorious, marvelous, tremendous surprise! Oh, my, what a surprise!"

It was Boggle, of course, standing atop the uppermost point of Krooom's nose horn, waving his splinted wing in the air. Directly below him, clinging to the horn, his face showing his wonderment at what he was seeing, was William — a flesh and blood William — who was very excited.

"William! Oh, William!" Lara cried.

"You're not just a skull any more, William!" Barnaby cried.

The twins leaped from their seats and ran to greet their cousin just as Krooom stopped nearby and the boy leaped nimbly down. The cheering that rocked the room

became even louder and more joyous when Mag Namodder announced that the destruction of King Thorkin had broken the Spell of *Mondu* he had placed on so many people over the centuries. All those who had been reduced to skulls had been restored to healthy living beings at the moment of Thorkin's destruction.

At last the hubbub died away as Mag Namodder faced the room and raised a hand for silence.

"The events of this momentous day are not yet completed," she said. "For those who gave their lives in the effort to become free of Thorkin's tyranny — heroes such as Trooom and Kreee and many others — memorial statues of each will be erected in our parks, so that we will never forget the supreme sacrifice they made.

"Furthermore," she went on, "I have already initiated the most expansive spell I have ever cast. It will take a day or two — or perhaps even three — to take effect. When it does, all the iron torques that the residents of our worlds have been required by King Thorkin to wear will vanish. No longer will anyone in Upperland or Twilandia ever have to wear anything around his neck unless he chooses to do so."

Loud cheering broke out at this and then quickly dwindled as it became obvious that Mag Namodder was not yet finished.

"Finally," she said, "and equally momentous for all, the tyranny of King Thorkin is over and now, at last, the rightful heir to the throne may be coronated."

Mag Namodder reached out and took Lara's hand and brought her to her feet to stand beside her. She gently touched her index finger to Lara's forehead. There was a bright flash and then a magnificent crown of gold and glittering diamonds and rubies and emeralds and other gemstones appeared on Lara's head.

"Lara," the Forest Witch said, "as firstborn of King Beyon, you are now the rightful ruler. The evil King Thorkin is dead. Long live good Queen Lara!"

"Long live the Queen!" shouted hundreds of voices in unison. "Long live good Queen Lara!"

Lara was overwhelmed and after a moment, everyone hushed to hear what their new Queen had to say.

"I . . . I thank you all, so very much," she told them. She looked at Mag Namodder. "But I know nothing about being a Queen. And, after all, Barnaby is my twin, born only a few minutes after me, so he certainly deserves to be King every bit as much. And what of our cousin, Prince Daw, who knows this land and its people so well and is certainly much more qualified to be the new monarch than either Barnaby or me? Is there anything that prevents all three of us to rule equally?"

There was a moment of silence as people looked at one another questioningly and then a voice in the crowd spoke up.

"There is no reason why not! None, none none! If that is truly what Lara, as rightful heir to the throne, desires." The man who spoke was a Gnome whose long red moustache was tied in an extravagant seahorse-shaped bow atop his bald head and both Lara and Barnaby gasped as they recognized Mr. Beadle.

"As a loyal official of the Thorkin realm, I have had access to all the records and bylaws housed in the collection of the Royal Library at Castle Thorkin. My loyalty is to the throne, rather than to the individual who occupies that seat. It is why I am one of those of Thorkin's force who remained here upon his death, for it is my responsibility to serve whoever newly occupies the throne. Serve," he said, "that's what I do. I serve the throne. Serve, serve serve."

He cleared his throat somewhat self-consciously and continued. "Now, then, I am the realm's foremost recognized authority on standards, charters, laws, writs, protocol, edicts, customs, registrations, genealogy and related subjects pertaining to both Twilandia and the countries of Upperland. I am. Indeed, indeed, indeed. Such matters have been my abiding interest and avocation for no less than eight hundred years, during my tenure as Gatekeeper of the Verdancia turnstile."

He paused and then smiled and bowed as a hesitant scattering of applause rippled through the crowd. He looked at Mag Namodder with one of his bushy red eyebrows raised in a questioning way.

"Continue," the Forest Witch said.

"Thank you," Mr. Beadle replied. "You may trust

that what I say here is entirely accurate. Accurate, accurate, accurate. The Royal Charter states quite clearly that, and I quote, '*On the occasion of the demise of the reigning monarch, power over the Realm shall be vested in the eldest offspring of the monarch or on several offspring or other blood relatives simultaneously, each with equal powers, should this be the wish of the rightful heir.*' Obviously, this is the case now. Yes, yes, yes!"

"That being the case," Mag Namodder said, "it is hereby proclaimed that henceforth Upperland and Twilandia shall be ruled equally by a triumvirate of these three, who are related by blood."

At this, all present jumped up and cheered and stamped their feet.

"Long live Queen Lara!" they cried. "Long live King Barnaby! Long live King Daw!"

And so it was . . . and thus came about the happiest time that anyone present had ever known.

20

The Departure

SO NOW our story is very nearly at its end. As joint rulers, Queen Lara and King Barnaby and King Daw governed Mesmeria and Twilandia very well for many many years and their subjects were happier than they had ever been before. By common consent of the three rulers, William was knighted and named First Prince of the Realm and became known and loved by all as Sir William.

Many years passed and Queen Lara grew into a very beautiful woman, while King Barnaby and King Daw and Sir William became tall, strong, handsome men. Time after time during this period, Lara and Barnaby and William made plans to return to the Other World to assure their families that they were still all right. But time after time urgent matters of state or emergencies of one kind or another intervened. Lara and Barnaby were only too aware of their responsibility to their subjects and they knew they could not just turn their backs and leave. Therefore, time and again they wound up postponing their return (much to the growing exasperation of William, whose responsibilities were minimal).

One day, when the four of them were relaxing and sipping tea in the Royal Garden after an especially trying time in settling a dispute between the Red Gnomes of Rubiglen and the Dwarfs of Selerdor, Queen Lara unexpectedly made an important decision.

"Regardless of whatever else occurs here," she said, addressing her twin and William, "we simply cannot any longer put off going home to see Uncle Danny and Auntie Alice and Mother and Father."

Barnaby and William looked at her and then at one another and nodded. They knew she was absolutely correct.

"Therefore," Queen Lara said, "I suggest that tomorrow we leave the Realm in the care of King Daw and we three take a brief trip back through the Verdancia Turnstile and let them know that we are safe and happy. We need only stay a short time and then we can come straight back to resume our duties."

Barnaby and William (especially William) thought this a wonderful idea. King Daw agreed to take good care of the Realm while they were gone. He was confident he could handle any problem that might arise in their absence and told them he would hold a Royal Banquet to celebrate their return.

The next day a large crowd gathered at the Verdancia Turnstile National Monument to see them off. Mr. Beadle was there as Head Gatekeeper and quite resplendent in a new suit, with his long red moustache bedecked with brightly colored bows and tied atop his head in the shape of a heart. Krooom was there, his scales newly waxed and glistening brightly. Boggle was on hand as well and there was a little note of sadness in his voice as he bade them farewell.

"Now you must be careful," the yellow bird warned. "Very careful. Extremely cautious. There are dangers out there. Oh, my, yes. Grave dangers. Awful perils. Do use great care and come back soon. Very soon. We will miss you. We will miss you a lot. Much. A very great deal. No one was ever missed the way you will be missed. Why, we'll miss you so much that —"

"Yes, Boggle," King Barnaby interrupted, "we get the picture. Thank you for your concern. We will miss you, too."

"Not to worry," put in Sir William. "We're not going into unknown territory. We know what's out there and we'll be all right, I assure you. And we certainly won't be gone very long."

(Which only goes to show that sometimes we can become overconfident, even when we feel assured we know what we are doing.)

Queen Lara and King Barnaby gave their bejeweled golden crowns to King Daw to keep safe for them until their return. Sir William, remembering his painful experience when he first entered this turnstile, gave his lucky silver dollar to Mr. Beadle to keep for him. Then, returning the waves of the crowd, one by one — first Queen Lara and then King Barnaby and then Sir William — the three passed through the turnstile.

Clickity-clickity . . .

. . . Clickity-clickity . . .

. . . Clickity-clickity.

Epilogue

SO THAT is the end of our story and now you can close this book and go to bed.

. . . What's that?

Some of you are saying you won't be able to sleep unless you find out whether or not Lara, Barnaby and William got home safely?

And do I hear others saying they want to know whether or not the three ever returned to Mesmeria?

Well, for those who are still curious, I suppose a brief report is possible here.

You must realize that Lara, Barnaby and William had no idea what to expect when they passed through the turnstile, but they certainly did not expect what occurred.

When the turnstile made its final clickity-clickity behind them, they discovered that nothing at all seemed to have changed from that moment so many years ago when they embarked on their great adventure. The turnstile was behind them on the pale green sand and William's boat was still beached just in front of them, not only with the cooler in it, but even with their oranges still inside the cooler. Most surprising of all was that they were little children again, just like they were when they had first entered the turnstile.

They discussed this turn of events and decided among themselves that possibly Mag Namodder had tried to help them by casting a spell to make this occur, though they could not imagine how that would be of any help. They then did the only reasonable thing under the circumstances, which was to head for Everglades City in William's boat, going back exactly the way they had come. As they passed through Loser's Creek they caught a brief glimpse of the big brown owl, but it flew off before they came near and they saw it no more.

When they reached the dock at William's house, Uncle Danny was in the yard trimming some shrubbery and Auntie Alice was picking weeds from her flower bed. They seemed wholly unchanged. The two grown-ups greeted them as if they had been gone no more than a couple of hours and William's father was pleased they had come back earlier than expected because there were some storm clouds building on the horizon.

The children had immediately begun chattering about their great adventure, but though the two grown-ups listened politely for a little while, soon Uncle Danny had excused himself, saying he had to get his trimming done before the storm hit. And Auntie Alice had listened politely a little longer and then excused herself to finish her weeding before the storm hit.

Deeply disappointed, hurt and even a little angry because it was obvious they hadn't been believed, the three had talked it over and decided they would just stay overnight and the next morning go back to Mesmeria where they could be themselves again and be shown some respect.

What a shame! I truly dislike having to tell you this, but that's not what happened.

That evening the storm hit — a very severe Florida storm of lashing winds and furious rains accompanied by thunder and lightning. It lasted for three days, uprooting numerous palm trees and causing considerable local flooding. And when it was over and the children finally set out again for Loser's Creek, the waters of the Barron River and the bays and the passageways were filled with storm debris — branches and

leaves and fallen trees. William found it necessary to maneuver the boat slowly and very carefully. It took quite a long while before they finally crossed the little hidden bay and entered the mouth of Loser's Creek. They found it almost impassable. Taking turns, they used Uncle Danny's machete to reopen the passage. Even though they worked steadily, it took them quite a long while to work their way back through the dark green tunnel to where they thought the entrance to the very dark tunnel should be, but they couldn't find it. Everything seemed changed and even the owl was gone.

Now, I suppose you know that when things go wrong, some people change for the better and some for the worse. That's what happened then among these three children and I think maybe you'll be able to understand this better if I repeat for you the conversation the three had.

"Oh, dear," Lara said, her eyes brimming, "we've lost it. We'll never be able to find the turnstile again."

"We'll find it, Lara," Barnaby replied. "Won't we, William?"

"I guess we can keep on looking for it," William responded, but he didn't sound very confident. "It's got to be here somewhere . . . if it really exists."

"What do you mean, if it exists, William?" Lara was frowning. "You know it exists. You do!"

"Well," her cousin shrugged, "I guess I'm just not so sure anymore. Not with all the queer things that've been happening." He shook his head and sighed. "Even if it was real, I don't think we'll ever find it again."

"Of course we will," Barnaby put in quickly. "We have to. Our people need us in Mesmeria and Twilandia. We've got to get back." He paused and when he spoke again, his voice had taken on a more reasoning tone. "Listen, William, we may not be able to find this turnstile, but don't forget, there are four others somewhere. Maybe we can find one of them."

"I still don't think we'll ever get back to Mesmeria again," William persisted in a dejected way. "If there actually is such a place." He sounded even less convinced than before and his words caused Lara to begin crying silently.

"Even if there is a Mesmeria," William continued, "I'm not sure I want to go back." He paused and then added defensively, "Maybe my mom and dad are right. Maybe we just imagined it all and it never really happened." He pulled the cord, starting the outboard motor, and headed the boat back toward home.

"It did so happen!" Barnaby flared, shouting to be heard over the sound of the motor. "It happened and we all know it, and I do want to go back. Don't you, Lara?"

His twin nodded and wiped her runny nose on her sleeve. They were all quiet for a while and then, I'm happy to report, Lara suddenly smiled through her tears. She leaned close to her twin brother and spoke in his ear.

"Don't fret, Barnaby," she said. "Now I know what we can do. Queen Enna — I mean, Mother — came into this world through the Twilandia turnstile. She must still know where it is. All we have to do is ask her.''

That's exactly what they did as soon as they got back to Chicago and I'll even go so far as to tell you that before they were reunited with their mother, a very remarkable thing happened.

But, of course, that's another story.

The End